Badtime Stories

Stories

William Marquess

Fomite

Burlington, Vermont

ISBN-978-1-947917-24-8
Library of Congress Control Number: 2019952762
Fomite
58 Peru Street
Burlington, VT 05401
www.fomitepress.com

For the nurses

I tell the tale that I heard told.

Mithridates, he died old.

A. E. Housman

Thanks, again, to Marc and Donna; to my Friday morning comrades at the Burlington Writers Workshop; and to my students, who have often been my teachers.

CONTENTS

Night Train

"Again," she said. "Again!"

He rose behind her, pulled her close, then flung her forward with all his skinny might. The cold lights of town rushed up before her, her bright yellow hair streamed out behind, and she screamed with delight. Then she fell back in his arms.

"Again!" she cried, and he pulled back the swing to give her another go.

It was late March in Burlington, and high school was on spring break, though nothing like spring had yet surfaced in northern Vermont. Her fingers were freezing in her mother's old red woolen mittens as she clung to the swing set chains. Earlier that night, she had sat with this boy for the first time.

"Shmoo," he said.

"What?" she said.

"Shmoo. Fizzlemug. Roustabout."

"I'm sorry? I didn't catch that."

"Matchstick, foosh, and blues magoos."

It was one a.m., at Denny's. The fluorescent light made everything too bright, too clean, too sheer with sharp edges. Maybe that was why she couldn't follow what he was saying: her eyes were so overstimulated that her ears had gone limp. Maybe it was the coffee buzz. Or maybe it was the fact that he always whispered, whispered and lisped. Maybe he whispered *because* of the lisp. She just wanted to understand.

A server came over — a tired-looking twenty-something whose laminated name tag said "Sally." "What can I do for you?" she said.

He brushed snarly dark curls out of his eyes. "Kzzee fee," he said.

"Excuse me?"

The girl pointed at the menu. "I think he said, 'Kids Eat Free.'"

"Right. So?"

He held out his hands, palms up.

Sally had had this conversation before. "You," she said, "are definitely not a kid."

"But *she* is." He gestured to the girl. "She's a mere babe in the woods." The girl was fifteen, and he was a year or two older.

"She's as tall as you are!"

He said, "Height is not a reliable measure of age."

Sally groaned. "Unless you have an ID that shows she's under ten, *and* your child or legal ward, everybody at this table is a paying customer."

"Oh," he said, "she's not my child. That would be weird."

Sally looked at her order pad. "So what can I do for you?"

The girl said, "Two eggs on toast, poached, and coffee, black."

"And for you, sir?"

"Hot chocolate," he said. "Mit schlag."

Sally looked at the girl, who said, "He wants whipped cream."

When Sally walked away, he turned to the girl and said, "'Coffee, black.' You are such a poser."

She shrugged. "At least I speak English."

He shrugged back, and returned to studying the menu. "Hey, I should have had the Birthday Special."

"Is it your birthday?"

He looked at her cross-eyed. "It *could* be," he said.

They had been to an all-ages show at Nectar's. When they came out on the sidewalk, under the solemn street light, she looked up and down the block and said, "This town is so lame. There's nothing open after midnight." She should have been home an hour ago.

"Zay dez," he said.

"What's that?"

He nodded down South Winooski Avenue. "There's Denny's."

She looked at him. Was he serious? She had been to Denny's — who hasn't been to Denny's? — but not in years. It was too riffraffy for her parents. Not that *they* would ever say that. In fact, her father was proud of being a small-town Vermonter, salt of the earth. But they both had jobs at the university, and her mother kept him on a low-sodium diet.

And then he took off. The girl hoped he was eating pretzels somewhere.

The guy was serious about Denny's. It was a hike, down past the washed-out shopping plaza and the interstate access. He didn't have a car. But what are a couple of miles in the dark, when you're fifteen, with a boy, and it's 1 a.m.? Her head was a lit match.

Sally brought their items. His *schlag* was already crumpled. Her eggs looked sad on their little raft of toast.

She took a bite. "It needs something," she said.

"Razzmatazz," he said.

"You have GOT to speak up!" she said.

"Razzmatazz!" he shouted. "That's what it needs!"

"Oh," she said.

From his coat pocket he pulled a cheerful little bottle of Texas Pete's Hot Sauce. "Never leave home without it," he said. It was just what she needed.

After a while, the bell over the door to the parking lot rang, and two guys walked in — Breiner and Ronan. She recognized them from school, but they had never spoken to her. Like the boy, they were a year ahead of her. They slid into the booth, Breiner next to her. They were both tall and thin, like the boy, with scruffy dark hair and thrift-store coats that didn't look warm enough for the final throes of winter in New England. Ronan looked at her across the Formica table with widened eyes. "What have we here?" he said.

"Nonnayer beezax," the boy said. He wiped some whipped cream from his long nose.

"It is *so* my beeswax," said Ronan. "My friend is hanging out with a new friend, and he doesn't even introduce her to his old friends? It's downright unfriendly."

The boy sighed. "Babe in the Woods," he said clearly. Then he added, "Ronan."

"And Breiner," said Breiner.

Breiner had a car. He dropped them off downtown. But they didn't want to go home yet.

They wandered toward the lake, as people do. On the way, they lingered at the big construction site where the mall used to be. That crypt had been leveled, and now a chunk of prime downtown real estate lay empty, waiting for the city to decide its fate. A private developer was proposing a huge complex of glass and steel, offices and apartments and shops in twin 14-story towers. It would need public money, and also a vote to exempt it from the city's limit on the height of structures. Not that Burlington was a city city; it was still College Town through and through. But its six square blocks of boxy downtown buildings gave it a little urban core.

The mayor was pushing for the development; he said it would bring trade and vitality. The girl's mother, who taught Environmental Studies at the university, was leading the opposition. It would cast dark shadows downtown, she said, create yet another playground for the wealthy, and line the developer's pockets with public cash.

They stood at the chain-link fence and peered into the arc lights. A full city block of mud and gravel was dotted with yellow back-hoes and tractors. They looked like the dinosaurs just before the meteor hit.

"Ex-two-twenty," he said.

"What?"

He pointed a bony ungloved hand at the nearest dinosaur. "That's an Ex-two-twenty. Best excavator for the money, bar none."

"How do you know?"

"That's what my dad does. In fact, if I'm not mistaken, that's his rig right there. He taught me to drive that thing. He wants me to work for the company." He shook his head. "No freakin' way."

He paused for a long moment. "Anyway, his company has this job. Or they would have it, if the protest hadn't gummed up the works."

"It has to be voted on!" she said. "The proposal is way too big, and there's not enough affordable housing!"

"How do you know?"

"That's what my mom does." She explained, and they fought for a while in an amiable way. The Ex-two-twenty sat precariously near the edge of a big muddy hole in the ground. But that's what excavators do.

They strolled on down to the waterfront boardwalk and looked out over the steaming lake. Along the rocky beach below them, someone had stacked up heaps of loose stones in clusters, like tiny Italian hill towns just waiting to be abandoned. There were dozens of these ragamuffin sculptures all up and down the shore.

"Nicodemus, Rastus, and Reeseman," he said.

"What?"

"The dude who builds those things," he whispered, "says they're actually messages from outer space. He says aliens direct him to the perfect rocks and then tell him how to stack them just so."

"Really?" she said.

"Maybe."

They walked on, to Perkins Pier. Beyond the empty boat slips, a little play area lay beneath a stand of skeletal oaks. After her solo ride, they sat on two swings, side by side. He fired up a cigarette. She loved the curl of acrid smoke that rose in the varnished dark.

From the pier came the steady clang of an empty flag pinion in the breeze, counting the frozen seconds. A freight train ghosted slowly by, sounding its doleful horn.

She wondered out loud, "Why is there a train at 2 a.m.? Why is it so slow? What does it carry?"

"Nitroglycerin," he said. "It's safer in the middle of the night. That's why it's so slow. If it jiggled too much, it would blow us all to smithereens." He spoke more clearly out here.

"Really?" she said.

"Fake news!" he said. "Actually, I have no idea. But we don't know that it's *not* nitro."

She bopped him on the leg.

"Mittens?" he said. "How old *are* you?" He started pumping his legs. "Bet I can go higher than you."

"Oh, I am the queen of this," she said. She started pumping hard. They rose and rose. The swing set creaked, one metal leg jumping out of its concrete hole. They kept rising. He shouted "Geronimo!" and let go, flying out over the wood mulch, onto the asphalt path by the lake. For a few long seconds, he didn't move. She stopped her pistoling legs, jumped off, and rushed to him just as he was getting up into a crouch. Even in the dark, she could see that his palms were bleeding. The blood looked black.

"Are you OK?"

"No, I'm screwed! Futhermuck!" He shook his hands and winced. And then he grinned. "But I won, right?"

She walked him to the apartment building where his family lived, down on Pine Street, right at the foot of her neighborhood. She had been inside the complex once, years before, with a classmate after school. She remembered seeing, on a white window ledge, the perfect circle left by a coffee cup, smudged by time. On the kitchen wall, telephone numbers were scribbled right in the paint, next to the spot where the landline used to hang. She was thrilled by these things.

He didn't invite her in—of course. It was 3 a.m., and his family was asleep. At the door, he said, "Jezelmehat."

She said, "Yeah! OK!"

Later, lying awake in her quiet room, she regretted the exclamation marks.

She just wanted to be good at something. Some people played guitar; some people made straight As; some people sailed through the Canyon at the skate park without ever falling. She couldn't carry a tune, and her grades were not so hot. She set her sights on mastering the skateboard.

Her father had given her the board for her thirteenth birthday, three months before he left for good. He taught her the two things he knew. One was how to pick the board up from the ground by pushing down with one foot on the tail so that the head popped into your hand. "Cool, huh?" he said.

The other thing was how to leave the board when she was done using it: always with the wheel-side up. "When I get home from work," he said, "I don't want to pull a Dick Van Dyke." Whatever that meant.

She practiced and practiced—first in the driveway, then on the sidewalk, then, when she could get a ride, at the skate park by the lake. But she kept falling. She wobbled even on the straightaways. She never mastered an ollie. One day at the park, she told a fellow boarder that she really didn't belong there.

"Hey, it's cool," he said. "I suck, myself." She watched him for a minute. It was true: he *did* suck. She felt better. She just needed to keep practicing.

But she didn't get any better. She wobbled, she fell, she collected bruises and scrapes. Her father was gone by now. Winter was beginning, and the crowd at the skate park was getting sparse. A different goal blossomed in her mind.

Maybe she could be good at boys.

Not that this came easily. She had always been tall for her age, and gawky. In grade school, boys flocked to the cute little girls like her friend Addie; they did not want to look up at potential paramours. In junior high, a more crucial problem emerged: she had no breasts. This was one of the reasons her friendship with Addie went south: Addie couldn't stop talking about boobs and bras, and the girl just didn't want to hear about it anymore. Too tall, too flat, too quiet for the squealers: seventh grade was a dry season.

Within a year, though, something miraculous happened: some boys didn't seem to care. They welcomed her at the skate park; when it rained, they sat with her under the shelter, and shared their Nalgene bottles; they smuggled her into shows at Nectar's, and passed her illegal beers. Some of them didn't care if she didn't say much. Some of them wanted to kiss her, and more. And that was okay with her.

But that wasn't what it meant to be good at boys. Anyone could do that. To make a guy love her—to get under his skin—to make him long for her—that's what she wanted.

She didn't remember a moment when they met. They had always been at the same schools, but he was a year ahead, which might as well have been another world. She had seen him get off the school bus at the apartment complex down the hill, another foreign world, far from the neat little single-family homes of Louise Street. And then he was always at the skate park that summer and fall when she was fifteen, tall and thin in his black jeans and black T-shirt, cutting the air like a blade. Watching him gave her hope that her own gangly limbs could be gathered and mastered someday.

One afternoon in March, he tick-tacked over to her.

"Nize tee," he said. "Classic." His nod at her Pink Floyd shirt gave her context. She said "Thanks," and crossed her arms over her chest.

"Wanna come see the Cakes?"

Whatever the question meant, she felt like saying yes.

He shouted, "Breiner!" From across the park another tall skinny dude came clattering on his board, pulling into sudden silence right before them.

"Put on a comp for my friend."

Breiner nodded, and took her name.

Then the first guy looked off toward the parking lot, where a big red truck had just pulled up. His face darkened. A tall man in a construction company cap called up to the platform that it was time to go.

The boy stared. The man shouted, "Get in the truck!" The boy's shoulders sagged. He walked off the platform, and got in the truck.

He was an imperfect gentleman. What would you expect from a guy who played bass in a band called The Urinal Cakes? Imperfection was their aesthetic. But she wasn't hung up on perfection. She liked his snaggle-tooth smile, his duck-footed walk, the skim-milk pallor of his forearms. He could wash his dark shoulder-length hair more often. If he didn't always return her calls and texts, she told herself people were too attached to their screens.

And if he sometimes sent her a sext of a long pale boner with the message "longing 4 U," she decided to take it as funny. She made sure to keep her phone always on her person, even at home. Her mother would freak.

Not that she and her mother saw much of each other these days. They had always been tense companions, long before her father left. The mother set rules; the daughter broke them. The mother grounded her, and the daughter found ways to get off the ground. She was limited to her room, and she climbed out her window onto the roof of the porch, then down a tree and away. She was given special chores, like daily watering of the community garden down the street; she bypassed the garden and went straight to the jungle gym, where some of her friends hung out. When her mother went through treatments for breast cancer, the daughter was required to spend time every day with their neighbor Evie, who coached her on her papers for English. She wrote screeds against her mother, and then stopped going at all. What was Evie going to do, snitch? Let her.

When her father was still with them, he mostly stayed out of the way. He tried to help; he played the Good Cop; but he knew he was out of his depth in this war between the two females of the house. After the cancer subsided, he left. His note said it was best for everyone. The mother got back to work. When the daughter started hanging out with boys, the mother gave her The Talk. When she started hanging out with *this* boy, the skateboarder from Jackson Terrace, who, according to the neighborhood gossip, had been picked up for breaking and entering, she said, "I forbid you to see that boy."

The daughter spoke the Rubicon words. "What are you going to do, hit me?"

The mother backed off. Maybe benign neglect was the only answer for now. She threw herself into organizing the opposition to the downtown development. The daughter came and went. There was uneasy peace.

Were the Cakes any good? Did it matter? They shredded, they clanged, they fa-la-lahed. They were brave enough to get on stage, and that was three-fourths of the way to being good.

One night in late March, as she walked home from town, she heard a roaring behind her, like a jet liner cleared for takeoff. Not until he pulled up beside her did she realize it was the sound of a board on a rough asphalt street.

"Dude," she said, "I hope you're not planning to be a private eye."

He smiled the snaggle-tooth smile, shrugged, and pushed off again. When he got to the corner, he picked up the board, carried it across the intersection, and threw it down again with a shoveling motion, so he had to run to jump on.

The Ex-two-twenty was operated by a key, just like any car or truck. The key hung behind Cora's counter in the front room, so a driver could snag it in the morning and hang it on its hook at the end of the day. Then Cora took inventory, making sure all the keys had come in. The boy knew, because he had been there, waiting for his father, when she was closing up. He saw the numbered hooks. His father's, earned by dogged longevity, was #1. As his father took a final leak and Cora bundled up to face the cold, he saw how easy it would be to lift that key before they all walked out to the parking lot.

His father had taught him how to start the rig, to operate the scoop, to get the heavy treads moving.

Now, in the weird brightness of the arc lights, he said, "Mayzhuryurdoorizzopen."

"Oh, don't worry," she said. "My door is open." She was hanging halfway out of it. The rig was just three feet from the edge of a fifty-foot pit, at the bottom of which shone a murky pool of indeterminate depth. The cab was strangely quiet. It was after 2 on a Wednesday morning. There had been no security around to see them scale the chain-link fence. Who was going to steal one of these rigs, even with a key? They maxed out at 5 mph. The get-away chase might be awkward.

The key fit like a charm, and the engine chugged to life on the first turn. It roared like a woolly mammoth and shook like a sonofabitch. It gave her gravy bones.

"This is insane!" she shouted.

He looked at her with his tenderest grin. Then he eased off the clutch, and the Ex-two-twenty lurched into motion.

"Smaug!" he shouted.

"Shiiiit," she cried.

They jumped, left and right, and landed in the mud at

the edge of the pit, where they both lay on their sides to watch the Ex-two-twenty roll over the edge. They heard a series of clangs as it banged down the pit wall, then a thudding splash and a couple of shudders. Then silence.

He stood, and whooped. She did her Jewish banshee. They glommed into a muddy hug. Then they laughed and laughed, as if there would be no end of laughter.

The next day after school, she went with her mother to see the site. A small crowd watched a crane drag the muddy and mangled excavator out of the pit. Her mother clicked her tongue.

"Isn't this a good thing?" the girl asked.

"We want to beat them the right way," her mother said. "This will just cost more, and where does the money come from? The taxpayers."

The boy was not in evidence. Off to one side, under a hard hat, his father glowered.

The girl walked down to Denny's that night, thinking she might see the boy, who hadn't responded to her texts. Or maybe Breiner and Ronan. But no. It was empty as a Denny's on a Wednesday at midnight. She ordered coffee, black. She said to Sally, "Did you hear about that big rig that went into the pit at City Place?"

Sally said, "Stupid kids."

"How do you know it was kids?"

"Who else would do something like that?"

"Why is it stupid?"

"That's somebody's *job* they trashed. Somebody's livelihood. Their rent, their children's dinner."

"But it's a terrible development!" the girl said. "It's, like, ginormous! Way taller than anything else in town! It's going to be full of fat cats, and shops and restaurants we can't afford!"

"Maybe so. But somebody's going to work in those shops and restaurants, right? Somebody's going to deliver stuff to them, and do the maintenance, and open the doors for the fat cats. And somebody's going to pay them."

The girl didn't see how she could argue with that. She sipped her coffee instead.

She and the boy broke up. Or they didn't, because hanging out doesn't lead to breaking up in the Neil Sedaka sense. You just stop hanging out. She saw him at the skate park on a blustery late-spring day—and almost didn't recognize him. He had shaved his head. He looked like a scalded cat. She said what's up, he said not much. Then he paused and said, "I'm dropping out." His elocution was impeccable.

She said, "Yeah?"

"Yeah. I'm seventeen, you know? I got better things to do."

She nodded. She didn't know what to say to a scalded cat.

He tossed his board into motion on the smooth platform, and ran to catch up with it.

She kept going to Denny's. The coffee was cheap, and nobody told her how many sugars she could have. She liked the long walk on those cool spring nights. She liked wearing her father's old flannel shirts. She liked watching Sally at the counter.

It was lonely here. She was probably flunking out of school. She didn't care. She had had her moment.

In the plate-glass window, a pair of tail lights pulled out of the parking lot, easing into traffic. She put her fingers to the glass.

"Again," she said softly. "Again."

LARIBOISIÈRE

On the second night in Paris, Ruth wound up in the hospital with a racing heart. She hadn't slept in three days now—the nervous night before leaving, the transatlantic flight, and the first night after arrival. When Mac found her at the window of their room at 4 a.m., red-eyed and naked, he insisted that they go to the hospital, just to be safe.

God, she thought, I've blown it now.

He was prepared to find a cab at the Gare du Nord and ask for the closest emergency room, but she said no, it's just around the corner. She knew from her college year in Paris, nine years before, when she lived in this neighborhood. They walked the surreal empty rue du Faubourg Poissonnière, under ochre street lights. The August heat had broken; it was almost cool. Mac draped his windbreaker over her shoulders. Was she in her right mind? Maybe not, but there it was, right around the corner: l'Hôpital Lariboisière.

It might have been a beautiful place, this hospital—a great arched entrance with an expanse of green courtyard beyond—but right now Mac and Ruth went straight to "Urgences," a wall of concrete with automatic glass doors and fluorescent lights that were far too bright. Ruth wanted to speak French with the woman at the counter, but Mac leapt to English.

"Her heart is racing," he said. "We need a doctor soon."

Amazingly, they saw a doctor soon. It being August, the French were out of town; the place was mostly empty. The doctor, a tall, dark-haired woman in a white lab coat, looked far too young for the job. Maybe that was why she was stuck with the graveyard shift in ER. She took Ruth's pulse by hand—two fingers to her wrist—and said, "You're right: your heart is racing. Why?"

"I wish I knew," said Ruth. With her slightly hooked nose, pale round face, and dark-framed glasses, she looked owlish even at twenty-nine. Crinkly chestnut hair sprang out in dishevelment.

"This is not the correct answer," the doctor said.

Ruth thought, I know! I know! She was embarrassed into silence.

The doctor said, "This does not happen at home, in America?"

"No. Well, sometimes."

The doctor looked puzzled, but went on. "You do not have a history of cardiac crisis?"

"No." Ruth's voice trailed off. She raised both hands like flightless wings.

The doctor said, "But?"

"No but."

"No but?"

"Just no."

"OK." The doctor's "k" rhymed with "eye." She looked at Mac, a lanky, sandy-haired man in cargo pants. "How many coffees have you taken today?"

Why was she asking Mac? He said, "Um, a lot."

"What is a lot?"

Was she asking what "a lot" means? Or how many coffees he meant by "a lot"?

"Beaucoup," he said.

The doctor frowned.

Ruth said, "Well, there was that terrible stuff at the Place du Tertre."

The doctor said, "You ordered coffee at the Place du Tertre?" As if to say, well, what did you expect? She started taking notes on a little pad.

"And then there was the good coffee at that café in the seizième."

The doctor looked up at Ruth's sudden use of French, as if the rules were changing. She was having none of it.

"Why go to the sixteenth?" Tourists almost never went there; it was all posh apartment buildings and ladies walking sausage dogs that were wearing doggy sweaters.

"For the Maison Balzac."

"Ah," the doctor nodded, as if this made perfect sense. "And then?"

"And then there was the café at that terrace place," said Mac.

"Terrace place?" the doctor asked.

"La Samaritaine," said Ruth.

"Ah yes," the doctor said, "Beautiful view."

"N'est-ce pas?" said Ruth. She couldn't help herself.

The doctor frowned again. "And then?"

"And then we split up," said Mac.

"You split up?"

"Not as in 'we broke up,'" he said. "We're still together."
He pointed to his paper engagement ring. She looked at
him as if she should be taking his pulse, too. "It's temporary," he said.

"And then?" she said to Ruth.

"Well, I had a cappuccino at a café near the Porte St.
Martin," she said.

Mac said, "You did?"

The doctor asked, "Why were you at the Porte St.
Martin?" Another unusual location for a tourist.

"I got lost," Ruth said. "I sat in a park for a while." She
felt as if the doctor knew that while in the park, she sat on
a bench and sobbed for fifteen minutes. "And then," she
said, "I got a cappuccino."

The doctor nodded. "Is that all?"

"Well, I also got a glass of white wine."

Mac said, "You did?"

The doctor said, "I mean, is that all the coffee?"

Mac said, "Don't forget the coffee they gave us on the
plane, just before arriving."

Ruth looked at him as if to say, Whose side are you on?
But the doctor marked it down.

"How many does that make?" Ruth asked.

The doctor counted, starting with the thumb. Fingers multiplied. Then she looked up and said, "Beaucoup."

Ruth thought this wasn't fair — but she was in no position to cry foul. She asked, "So?" She braced herself for the lecture on excessive caffeine.

"So we admit you."

"You do?"

"Yes! Your heart is racing! We calm it, no?"

"No!" Ruth said. "I mean yes!"

Then the doctor got them to watch as she drew something on her pad. A picture of a coffee cup, with a sweet little curlicue of steam. A circle around it. A diagonal line through it. She said, "I send this to the nurse."

When the doctor left them to wait for an assistant who would direct them to admissions, Mac said, "You gotta love nationalized medicine."

They put her in a shared room, just big enough for two single beds, divided by a silver nylon curtain. Ruth got the bed closest to the door; the other bed was next to the only window, still dark at 5 a.m. Before settling in, she stole a look behind the curtain. On the pillow, dimly lit by the perpetual light from the hall, lay a dandelion puff of white hair. The name card at the foot of the bed read "Dupont."

Mac was not allowed to stay: visiting hours began at 1 p.m. He said, "I'll be back before you can say 'déjà vu'."

She wanted to ask him more — what would he do, alone in Paris? — but a nurse shooed him out. The nurse looked around thirty, dark-haired and compact, with a name tag that said "Rivière." Ruth wanted to talk, to establish that she was capable in French, but the nurse shushed her with a finger to the lips and a look at the curtain behind which her roommate slept. She gave Ruth a pill — "to sleep," she said in English — and a tiny cup of water.

Ruth swallowed it, knowing it would do no good. Her door was open to the brightly lit hall, where nurses and orderlies bustled past, pushing carts. From behind the curtain, not six feet from her head, some kind of respirator wheezed. Or was that just Madame Dupont?

She was probably fine. It was all that coffee. And the jetlag. And then yesterday had been such a whirlwind, capped by Mac's paper-ring proposal. She was probably fine.

She heard a voice — low and hoarse, an old voice. "Mon dieu," it said. "Mon dieu." It came from behind the curtain. Or did it say "Matthieu"?

Ruth pushed the button to call the nurse, who arrived almost immediately. "The woman, there," she said in French, pointing to the curtain, "she called for something."

The nurse took a look, then reappeared at Ruth's bedside. "She sleeps, madame," she said in French. "You should sleep, too." She turned and left the room.

"Madame?" Ruth thought. "I'm no madame! I'm no older than you!" Maybe this was just protocol.

Behind the curtain, the voice spoke again. "Mon dieu," it said. "Mon dieu." Or maybe "Matthieu."

Next thing she knew, there was daylight, there was a different nurse taking her vitals, there was a game show on the television high on the wall, visible from both beds.

She couldn't see her roommate behind the curtain, but she heard the tinny laughter from the speaker built into the other bed's controls. Mon dieu, she thought, and drifted off again.

It wasn't really sleep; it was Benadryl, and she was Benadrunk. Before long, there was something like lunch on the table that swung over her bed, and they let her ignore it. She was supposed to sleep. And then there was Mac on the edge of the bed. There were red roses in a drinking glass on her table. There was a plate full of something steamy in his lap.

"Couscous!" he said. "You don't get this much in Bristol, Vermont." He pronounced it "cows-cows." "Leave it to the French," he said, "to have really good food in their hospitals. Want some?"

Ruth shook her head. Rivière, standing at the foot of the bed with a clipboard, said in French, "That's not couscous. I'm Algerian, I know. That is cafeteria slop." Ruth laughed, and Mac said, "Hey, no fair!" Rivière smiled before moving on.

Ruth asked, "So where have you been this morning?"

"I walked down to the river," he said, "because, well, it's the river. Then I wandered over into that neighborhood behind the dinosaurs." The day before, he had stood rapt before a stegosaurus at the Museum of Natural History. "And I wound up in the coolest little park—les Arènes de Lutèce." He pronounced it "areens," but Ruth knew what he meant—a park built on the ruins of a Roman arena. "There's not much to it now," he said, "just a crumbling wall and the round shape where the arena was. But you can totally see how it would have been, full of Christians and lions or whatever. Like my daddy always said, you just have to imaginate."

She smiled. Who was this strange and wonderful man who came to Paris with her?

"So I sat there long enough to have a cigarette, and then it was time to head back up here."

"You what?"

"Headed back up here."

"No," she said, "the cigarette part. Since when do you smoke?"

"Since I was twelve," he said. "Only I hardly ever do, now."

She shook her head. "I love it," she said.

"You do?"

"Yes! I mean no, it's a filthy habit, but I love knowing that you have one. I thought you were Mister Clean."

He tweaked his invisible Snidely Whiplash mustache. His beard, if he had one, would have come in reddish. He was ruddy and loose-limbed as the Scarecrow in Oz.

She said, "Isn't it disgusting? Drawing smoke into your lungs?"

"Actually, no, it's pretty wonderful. It makes me feel more alive. Though I know it's killing me. But don't worry, I can take it or leave it. I'll just have one every time I'm sitting in an ancient Roman arena in Paris."

"So now what are you going to do?"

"I'm going to sit here with you. I brought a book." He

patted the oversized pocket on the thigh of his cargo pants.

"Of course you did." He was, after all, a librarian. "But you're in Paris!" She waved in the direction of the window, which they couldn't see because of Madame Dupont's curtain. "You can't sit in a hospital all day!"

"Just watch me," he said. He pulled out his book. "It's called *Permanent Parisians.* It's about all the famous people buried in Paris cemeteries. Did you know that Truffaut is buried in Montmartre?"

That was one she knew. Nine years before, her French lover had taken her there not long before he left her sobbing in a little park.

Mac settled into the one chair, squeezed between the hall door and her bed. This gave her time to think about the work she wasn't doing. Classes at the university would be starting in ten days, and although she had done all the prep, she felt, as always, underprepared. She was here on a travel grant for young faculty; she was supposed to be visiting the new "eco-quarters" of Paris. She fretted at the classes coming up. How could she introduce them to Environmental Studies in just one semester? There were so many issues, so many examples she wanted to feature. One of them was this very city — how its infrastructure had been so badly abused in the past thirty years, since they moved the great central market, Les Halles, out to the suburbs.

She remembered the first — and only — time she discussed her teaching with her father, back when she was still a TA. They were in a bar on the Upper West Side, where he had taken an apartment after moving out of their New Jersey home. Rather than focus on his abandonment of her mother, she agonized over her new teaching assignment.

He said, "You're making it too hard, Ruthie. You just figure out what they want, and then that's what you give them."

"No, you don't," she said.

He gaped. "What do you mean?"

"You have to teach them to want something better."

He took a sip of his drink. "Good luck with that," he said.

After her mother acquiesced in the divorce — she should have sued for more — Ruth gradually fell out of touch. She was the only child. She wasn't Ruthie anymore. They both had new lives. She gave herself entirely to the new Environmental Studies program at the University of Vermont. That's where she met this sandy-haired librarian.

In the middle of the afternoon, she asked, "Mac, do you believe in God?"

He looked up from his book.

"Jeez, I don't know."

There was game-show chatter from behind the curtain, people passing in the hall. He went on.

"I mean, I don't *not* believe. Before I came up to your room today, I lingered in the hospital chapel, because I was early, and it's always open. That's a lovely thing, that it's always open. And it's really grand — great Gothic windows, you know, dark stone, stained glass. It makes you think how powerful belief can be. I know that a lot of people who are smarter than I am have been believers. But I just don't know. You know?"

She nodded. They had known each other for a year, lived together for six months, and never had this conversation.

He said, "What about you?"

She shifted her weight in bed. "I've always liked the story about the group of Jews in Dachau who put God on trial. It's the end of the day, and they're exhausted, sitting in a circle, in the dirt, tattered work clothes falling off their emaciated bodies—but they hold a proper trial, hearing all the evidence on God's behavior. And it's unanimous: they find God guilty." She paused. "Then a bell rings in the distance, and they all go off to evening prayer."

Soon, the doctor came by. Her white coat was crisper than it had been at 5 a.m. When did she sleep? She nodded at Mac, and spoke to Ruth in English.

"You sleep?"

"Yes," Ruth said, "I slept. Some."

The doctor took her pulse, again by hand, two cool fingers resting on Ruth's wrist. The skin of her hand was like opal. She wore no wedding band. Ruth watched her dark brown eyes for the results.

"Your labs are fine," the doctor said. "You seem to be OK."

"But?"

"Your heart is still too fast."

"So?"

Mac was watching silently. He had stood up when the doctor came in; now he was backed against the wall.

"I think you have RAS," the doctor said.

"RAS?"

"Romantic American Syndrome." The last word sounded like "seen-drum."

Mac laughed. Ruth wasn't sure it was funny.

"You come to Paris, it's supposed to be beautiful but maybe it's not, the weather is hot, the Parisians are disappeared, you drink coffee, a lot" — she smiled at Mac — "and maybe too much alcohol?" They hadn't mentioned the Calvados. "And your heart, that goes too fast."

Ruth bowed her head. Now would come the dismissal, the slap on the wrist.

Actually, the doctor was still holding her wrist. Her hand was still cool.

"So you stay again tonight."

"I do?"

"Yes. We want your heart rate slower."

A silence passed between the two women. Then the doctor looked at Mac. "Your fellow," she said, "he knows how to pass the time, no?"

Mac said, "I do."

Even Mac had to admit that the cafeteria soup for dinner was bland, and the bread was more than a little crusty. At seven, Rivière arrived for the evening shift. "August," she said. "We all work extra." She looked at the bowls on Ruth's table, still half-full of congealed soup, and grimaced. "Sunday night," she said. "The Sisters volunteer in the kitchen." She crossed herself. "They think you will be filled with nutritious devotion."

She cleared the table, and returned a minute later, holding a covered earthenware pot, which she handed to Mac. "Couscous," she said. "The real thing." Before he could even thank her, she said, "I have other patients. Microwave in the hall."

It was delicious. Afterward, Ruth asked, "So what will you do tonight?" Visiting hours ended at eight.

"I don't know," Mac said. "The city lies before me."

Only after he had gone did she realize that the television had been dark for some time. What was up with Madame Dupont?

Sometime in the night, she heard the voice again. She couldn't make it out; it was fainter now. But still it sounded serious. She punched the call button.

The nurse who came was not Rivière. Ruth responded to her in French. "Madame Dupont," she said, "was calling. Maybe she can't press the button? She needs help."

The nurse was a silhouette against the hallway light. "Elle n'y est plus, madame." She is no longer there. "Dormez." Sleep.

She slept. Or she visited the precincts of sleep. Shadows came and went. Hours passed. Morning light suffused the silver curtain between the two beds.

After breakfast—fresh bread now, with good butter and

jam, orange juice, but no coffee — a man appeared at the door. Fortyish, slender, with a dark well-trimmed beard and gold-rimmed glasses, he wore a dark sport coat and well-pressed slacks. He peered at Ruth, at the number on the door, at Ruth again. Then he seemed to register that there was another bed beyond the curtain, and he stepped into the room. "Excusez-moi, madame." He went behind the curtain. For several minutes, Ruth heard shuffling sounds; then he emerged, with a full canvas bag over his shoulder. "Pardon, madame."

As he was headed out the door, Ruth said, "Matthieu?"

He stopped, then frowned.

"Non," he said. "Didier."

Then he turned and went on his way.

Standing naked at the window of their lodging on the first night, Ruth can see two things. One is a plastic clam-shell pill dispenser, its numbered circular slots loaded with pills, a pill for each day of the month. It sits on her dresser in their apartment in Vermont. It is sitting there even now.

The other thing she sees is a young woman in jeans and a peasant blouse. It's a fine September day. The young woman — hardly more than a girl — carries a heavy-look-ing backpack over one shoulder. Her features are indis-tinct; Ruth sees her only from behind. But she is striding purposefully across a green campus, on her way to class. No wonder Ruth's heart is racing.

BADTIME STORY

Once there was a woman who sat by a window every day.

He is telling a story. His daughter interrupts.

On the Coast of Coromandel?

On the Coast of Coromandel, where the early pumpkins blow.

This is how all his stories start. He is sitting on the edge of her bed, on a hot September night, in a room so cluttered with clothes and books and toys that he could hardly find a path from the door to the bed. This is the Kingdom of the Only Child. His wife is downstairs in her study, saving the world.

Will you stay till I'm asleep?

We don't do that anymore, Sprout. You're a big girl now. You can go to sleep on your own.

Sometimes he calls her Bean. She gets her height from him; her mother is five foot three.

I don't want to be a big girl!

Sometimes he calls her Daddy's Little Monster.

Well, that's what happens when you eat your Cheerios.

She sighs a brokenhearted sigh, and pets the dog beside her. A big black Lab with a silver muzzle, he takes up two thirds of the bed.

Can Sloppy Joe stay?

You know he can't. He has his own bed.

Will you leave the light on when you go?

You'll sleep better in the dark.

No I won't.

He doesn't answer. Outside the open window, crickets scrape their bows. He and her mother have started calling this time of day "badtime." Their daughter seems intent on not sleeping. Some nights, after being put to bed, she gets up and microwaves a pizza. Some nights, she logs onto her father's computer, which is strictly forbidden. Some nights, she comes to his side of the parental bed and wakes him, looking for company. How can anyone else be asleep? She has been doing poorly in school, and her mother says it's because she's sleep-deprived.

Will you leave the hall light on?

OK, yes, the hall light can stay on.

This is not the deal he made with Ruth. No lights, she said, and he nodded. But in his mind he had his fingers crossed behind his back. Ruth is deep in her e-mail now, urging their neighbors to Say Yes to a Livable City By Voting No On The Downtown Zoning Ordinance. He volunteers for badtime so she can have this time for work. His job at the university library doesn't require any homework. And he likes telling stories. He'll come back and turn out the hall light before Ruth comes up to bed.

He clears his throat, and begins again.

On the Coast of Coromandel, where the early pumpkins blow, there was a woman sitting by a window.

When?

A long time ago.

Before I was born?

Before you were born.

Before you met Mom?

Yep.

Were you there?

You'll see.

She squirms. This is her unfavorite answer. He needs to get some traction.

It was a small apartment in the city, five floors up and no elevator. The window looked to the east, so it brightened her little apartment in the morning. The woman put a chair by it, and a little table, where she placed an electric teakettle.

Like ours?

Like ours. Only smaller. She lived alone. It was a hard time in her life. She had just finished college, and she didn't know what to do.

Why not?

She didn't know what she wanted. I mean, she knew she wanted buttered noodles and Phish Food, but that wasn't enough.

Why not?

She didn't know. But that's what people said.

People are goombahs.

You're right, people are goombahs. But that's what they said, and they said it so much that she started believing it. So it was a hard time.

Did she have a boyfriend?

Nope. She had boyfriends in college, but they were all beer and skittles. They smelled like blue cheese.

Yuck! Did she have a dog?

No Pets Allowed.

Her hand smooths the fur on Sloppy Joe's flank.

So what did she see from the window?

I thought you'd never ask. The window looked out on another building, thirty feet away. When she sat in her chair with her cup of tea, she could see into the windows across the alley.

How many windows? Could she see people? Who lived over there?

Hold your horses, Bean. All things in time.

A car slides by on their quiet street, blasting hip-hop, bass notes rumbling. It's too hot for mid-September in Burlington, but Ruth doesn't believe in air conditioning. Back when they first met, he found this charming, like her root-vegetable soups and her essential oils. He was pleased when they bought this old house close to town, with its narrow upstairs rooms, perfect for cold winter nights. But after a steamy August, he'd just as soon live in one of the sleek downtown condos Ruth is writing e-mails against. She says gentrification forces the poor out of the city. She teaches Environmental Studies at the university; she ought to know. Tonight, though, he wouldn't mind being part of the gentry, if the gentry have central air. He wipes a bead of sweat from his lip, and continues.

The woman could see two windows. One of them looked into an entrance hall, where she could see if anyone entered the apartment. The other, to the right from her perspective, looked into a bedroom.

How could she tell?

She could see the bed. And the man in the bed.

There was a man in the bed? All the time?

Yes, all the time.

Was he sick?

That's what it looked like.

What did he have?

She couldn't tell from that far away. His bed was on the far side of the room.

But you know, don't you?

He had — purple fever.

Is it bad?

The worst.

What does it feel like?

It's like — you know when Sloppy's sleeping, and he kicks his leg and yips? It's like that, only all the time.

She grips a handful of pelt. He goes on.

One day, the woman at the window saw someone else come into the man's apartment. A woman.

His girlfriend?

Yes. Well, no. It's his girlfiend, actually.

His girlfiend? What's wrong with her?

Nothing is wrong with her. She's just — she's — it's just a joke between them.

Some joke.

The woman at the window saw that the girlfiend was carrying a brown paper bag.

What was in it?

It was from a bakery.

Was it macaroons?

Pink and lavender ones.

Yum.

Also, a big cup of coffee.

Mister Yuck!

Well, he happened to like coffee. The way it steams when you put your nose in the cup.

He's a goombah.

Maybe so, but he was a thirsty goombah. The woman at the window saw the girlfiend enter the apartment, set the bag down on a table by the door, take off her coat — it was winter, and very cold — and then pick up the bag and disappear for a moment before reappearing in the bedroom window, like magic.

It's not so magical, Dad. It's just two rooms.

OK, so she reappeared like a person who walked from one room into another room. And now she had the macaroons and coffee on a tray.

She must have stopped in the kitchen.

You think?

She ignores the snark. Was he allowed to eat in bed?

Yep.

No fair!

It's a house rule: No food outside of the kitchen slash dining area. He keeps a stash of Cheez-Doodles in his study, which is what they call the room where he watches ballgames. He lets her have some if she wipes the orange dust off her hands before going back into the world. And if she roots for the Red Sox.

It's his own apartment. He can eat wherever he wants.

I want my own apartment!

The whiny thread in her voice is a good sign: it means she's getting sleepy.

I thought you didn't want to be a big girl.

I want to be a small girl with her own apartment.

As soon as you start bringing in the big bucks, Sprout.

He looks out the window for a minute, just a minute. He doesn't know where he's going with this. A whiff of compost rises on the late-summer air. Ruth makes them toss everything into that steaming box. The Bean used to love digging around in there, just to gross herself out. Off in the distance, the City Hall bell rings nine.

And then he hears a new sound: her steady breathing. Well, what do you know.

If he were to get the dog up now, that would ruin everything. He'll deal with it later. He turns out the light.

The next day, the woman at the window saw something new.

He perches on the edge of the bed, his legs all stuck to his trousers. This weather is making him crazy. Last night he slept on the living room sofa, because it's cooler downstairs. That is, he tried to sleep. He lay awake in the sweaty dark, listening to the drip of a leaky kitchen faucet. He's supposed to get that fixed. He forgot to go back and get Sloppy Joe.

The Bean is turned the other way, looking at the wall. This morning, when her mother did the wake-up shift, she discovered the dog in her daughter's bed, and so Sloppy has been exiled to the back hall. There's a perfectly good dog bed out there, where a sliding wooden lattice pens him in.

Don't you want to know what she saw?

She doesn't answer.

Well, OK, I guess I'll just go watch the ballgame. I thought you'd want to know.

Was it the girlfiend? She says this to the wall.

Yep.

On the Coast of Coromandel?

Where the early pumpkins blow.

Was Mister Yuck still in bed?

Yep.

So what's new about that?

The girlfiend had a plan.

What was it?

At first, the woman at the window couldn't tell. It was thirty feet away, after all.

She should get binoculars.

Wouldn't that be a little creepy?

Yeah! She turns to face him now.

He has been thinking about this all day. At dinner, when

Ruth talked about the Town Center campaign, how they're going to give the city back to the people, his mind wandered to the woman at the window. He picks up the story.

She didn't get binoculars. But she saw Mister Yuck sit up in bed when the girlfiend arrived. Then the girlfiend disappeared, not like magic, and reappeared in his room, and stood by his bed. The woman at the window could see him listening to her.

What was she saying?

The woman at the window didn't know. She took a sip of tea, and waited.

Didn't her tea get cold?

She liked it cold. More anticoagulants.

More what?

They make your blood run.

Whatever. Tell the story!

She put her tea cup down. She was worried. Mister Yuck had been in bed a long time now.

He has to get better!

Why?

Because the girlfiend needs him!

Well, she said some things, and after a while, he nodded.

And then?

And then—she moved his bed.

She what?

She moved his bed. She went around to the far side, away from the window, and started shoving. She had to put her back into it. Did I mention she was petite? But she was strong. She shoved his bed right across the floor.

So he got a ride?

Yes. He waved his hands in the air.

Can we do that?

He looks around the cluttered room. I don't think so, Bean. But this ride wasn't just for fun. The girlfiend had a purpose.

What?

At first, the woman at the window couldn't tell. But then she realized: the girlfiend was moving him closer to the window, so now he got all the light.

And the woman at the window could see him better, too?

Yes.

What did he look like?

He looked — tired. And bored. His heart was bored with his mind.

What does that mean?

It's a saying.

She pauses. And then?

That's it.

That's it? She moved his bed?

Um, yeah.

Well, that's a dumb story.

Everybody's a critic.

She turns back to the wall.

Say goodnight, Bean.

She usually says Goodnight, Bean and cracks up at her own joke. Tonight she says, I want Sloppy Joe.

He turns out the light, and lets her be. If she gets up in the night, he'll deal with it then.

The best thing about going to work these days is that the library is air-conditioned. At his lunch break the next day, he sits in the basement snack bar with Silverman, his comrade in Reference. It's cool as a meat locker down here. He gets out his PB & J and turns to Silverman, who is having a cup of soup from the kiosk.

Did you used to read to Willow?

Oh, yeah, every night.

Silverman is about fifty, a slight guy with a graying ponytail and kind eyes behind wire-rim glasses. His daughter is in her twenties now.

Like, what did you read?

You name it. When you read every night, you cover a lot of ground.

What worked best?

Happy endings. You've got to have a happy ending, that's just the deal. We had this big book of fairy tales, and Willow wouldn't let me go until she got her Happily Ever After.

But those endings are so bogus! I tried those with my daughter when she was younger. I mean, Little Red Riding Hood? She gets gobbled up! Hansel and Gretel escape the witch, but then they go back home to the father who ditched them in the woods! It freaked me out when I read that. Then, let's see, Rumpelstiltskin? The girl marries the King who threatened to kill her, and the little dude who spun the gold tears himself in two! Now *there's* a happy ending. And don't get me started on all the princesses: they wind up with those dimwit princes!

Silverman looks at him sideways. Are you OK, man?

Yeah, sorry. I haven't been sleeping well.

The next day, the woman at the window saw something new.

That's how you started last night!

I just wanted to see if you were paying attention.

So? Did the girlfiend visit him again?

Yep.

On the Coast of Coromandel?

Where the early pumpkins blow.

And his bed was by the window now?

Yep.

So?

He pauses, just to slow things down. Swim lessons usually tire her out, but tonight she's wired. Maybe it's the heat.

So — this time the girlfiend was carrying something.

What?

It was small. She put it down on the table by the door, and she took off her gloves and coat. She rubbed her hands, to warm them. The woman at the window could see the cold smoke of the outside air around her.

But what did she put on the table?

She picked it up, and disappeared from the window — not like magic, I know — and then she reappeared at the other window, by his bed.

Daddy! What is it?

When she sat down in the chair by his bed, she had this thing in her lap. She didn't seem to be doing anything. But the man was watching her intently. Everything got quiet.

There are peepers on the evening air. A garage door rattles shut across the street.

The woman at the window could see that the girlfiend's lips were moving.

It's a book!

Who told you?

What book is it?

It's — poetry, he says. It's — lullabies.

His daughter is quiet for a moment.

No, she says.

No?

Lullabies are for babies.

Oh. He looks at the dark outside. It looks back at him. He has messed this up. It's a runamuck computer, an interlibrary loan that won't come home. All he's got is a room full of straw.

So what do *you* think happens?

Mister Yuck gets up!

Really?

Yes! He gets up! He's tired of lying in bed all day.

What does he do?

First, he gets some cereal. With lots of milk, and two spoons of sugar.

And coffee?

She wrinkles her nose. OK, yes, coffee. He sticks his nose in the cup, then he pours it down his gullet. It makes his blood run.

And then?

He stays in his bathrobe. He reads the newspaper. She

holds up her hands in bed, rattles an invisible paper, and harumphs at the news.

He chuckles. She's good.

No laughing! This is serious.

Does he get dressed?

He *is* dressed! In his bathrobe! He's staying home.

What about the purple fever?

It's OK.

Did it go away?

She pauses. No. It doesn't go away. But you can live with it. You take two pills every day, and you listen to music, and you stop reading the news.

This is a good description of her mother, except for the stopping part.

What kind of pills? What kind of music?

Gummy pills. Boysenberry. And all the musics. David Bowie. The Kinks. Music from Big Pink.

She has just named her father's pantheon.

And then?

And then The End! She dusts her hands. Voilà! She knows that when you say it in French, it's really over.

Aren't we forgetting someone?

She pauses. The girlfiend?

Yes. He really wants to know.

She pauses again. I'm thinking. The next day, she comes over, and she's carrying . . . a backpack!

What's in it?

Her peejays! And her toothbrush! It's yellow.

She's spending the night?

It's a sleepover. They keep the kitchen light on. Over the stove.

Wow, that's a great story. He reaches for the lamp.

She stops his hand. Wait a minute. Aren't we forgetting someone?

He thinks. Oh, the woman at the window?

Yes, she says, drumming her fingers on her chin. What about her?

Well, when she sees that the girlfiend is moving in—

Wait, she's moving in? I thought it was just a sleepover.

Nope, she's moving in. She likes his bathtub.

She doesn't have a bathtub?

Just a dribbly shower.

Well, no wonder she's moving in. And the woman at the window?

Well, when she sees that the girlfriend is moving in, she sits up, and takes a long sip of tea—

Stop stalling.

She takes a long sip of tea—and then she goes to bed.

Just like that?

She was ever so sleepy. Say goodnight, Bean.

Didn't she brush her teeth?

Yes. She brushed her teeth first.

And put on her peejays?

And put on her peejays.

And lock all the doors?

She locked all the doors.

And checked her e-mail?

He wants to say there is no e-mail in Coromandel. But

he says, Yes, she checked her e-mail.

Did she get one from me?

Did she . . . ? Hmm, yes, I believe she did.

What did it say?

Well, you wrote it, you know what it said.

But I want to know if she understood it.

It said I love you. Yours truly, The Bean.

That's right! So?

So then she went to bed.

In the dark?

She liked it dark.

She's a goombah.

No, she's a smart girl. She knew she was safe, and there was sugar in the jar, so she could sleep like a tater-tot.

Did she figure out what to do with her life?

Now who's stalling?

I want the whole story!

But you never get the whole story, Sprout. You just get one day at a time.

That's what I hate about it!

Yeah, he says. Me too.

He turns out the light, and she doesn't protest. Maybe Silverman was right.

Downstairs, a thin line of light gleams under Ruth's door. He hears the clicking of the keyboard, words whickering out into the dark. He places a hand on the door. Then he walks down the hall, frees the dog from his pen, and takes him out for his nightly walk.

At ten o'clock it's still hot, and Sloppy wants to sniff everything. All the smells of the world are keener in the heat. Everyone seems to be outdoors. Evie and Leah are on their front deck, chatting quietly under the porch light. Evie waves. Down the street, the guy with the apple tree is picking up windfalls, using a flashlight to find them. In the park at the end of the block, a clutch of teenagers hovers by the jungle gym, smoking who knows what. How soon will the Bean be among them?

He and Sloppy make their usual circuit twice. If they stay out long enough, maybe the heat will break.

By the time they get back home, Ruth has gone to bed. There are no lights on upstairs. He pens the dog and uses the downstairs bathroom. Then he locks the doors, douses the lights, and lies down on the sofa, still in his T-shirt and shorts. The kitchen faucet is still dripping. He is still thinking about the woman at the window.

On the final day, she watched the girlfiend arrive, with nothing in her hands. She entered the apartment and said something to the air. She cocked her head. Something had changed. She didn't take off her winter coat, but hurried to the man's bed, and found that he wasn't moving. Purple fever is a fearful thing.

And then?

She took off her coat, and walked it to the coat tree in the hall. She stepped up to that window — the left-hand window — and she seemed to stare straight at the woman watching from across the alley. The woman's heart stopped.

But then she realized that the girlfiend was only looking at the world. And her face was wet with tears.

Then what did she do?

After a long moment, she disappeared, and returned
to the bedroom with a basin and a towel. She lowered
the sheets, removed the man's pajamas, and then, slowly,
with a large yellow sponge that she drew from the basin,
she bathed him. From time to time she dipped the sponge
into the basin. Then she toweled him dry, taking special
care with the toes.

And then she did the strangest thing. She undressed,
slowly—everything was slow—and stacked her clothing in a neat pile on the end of the bed. Sweater, blouse,
skirt, undergarments. She had an ordinary body—small
breasts, narrow hips. She lay down beside him. She
pulled up the covers. And then they were perfectly still.

The woman at the window stared. She didn't know
what to do.

What will she do with her life?

That's what she had to find out.

LETTERS TO YEZ

Dear Yez,

Is it OK if I call you that? "Yesualda" seems so formal—and I don't know how to pronounce it. But Yez is kind of like Pez—do you have those? You know, the little plastic things where you pull back Mickey's head, or Goofy's, and it gives you a treat? My dad gave me one of the Little Mermaid, she's my favorite character. I ate all the treats right away, one after another as Ariel served them up click click click, and my mom won't let me get more. But I'm holding onto Ariel. I love her red hair. Someday I'll fill her up again.

So my mom asked me if I wanted a pen pal in Kenya, and I said I don't know, and she said it would be a mitzvah. We don't go to temple or anything, but still, I know a mitzvah is good. She got me this stack of paper, and envelopes, and these cool international stamps—14 of them, enough to send one letter a week for the whole summer. I know it's really a way to keep me busy during vacation, but I said OK, as long as nobody reads what I write except for you, my pen pal. I could tell Mom didn't like that idea, she hesitated. But then she nodded. So, this is our first letter.

BTW, she says you probably don't know who Ariel is, or what Pez is, because they're "western" things, which sounds like Cowboys and Indians, but I don't think that's what she means. She says you probably get your food straight from a farm or a garden, not from a store. Dad says to her, "Have you been to Kenya lately?" And she gives him the Leave Me Alone look. She wants us to raise our own food from the new garden over in the park, when it's finished. Which is cool and all, but you can't fit a zookeeney into a Pez head. It's so much easier to go to Cumby's, and they have slurpees, too. Mom says slurpees are Not Food. But they taste good! I like cherry. But then my mouth and tongue get all red, and Mom yells at me when I come home. She says she doesn't yell, but I know yelling.

Let me know if you don't know about Ariel, and I'll tell you all about her.

So now I'm going to put your name and address on the outside, and seal it for nobody but you. Write back soon!

Your friend,
Harper

Dear Yez,

How are you? Did you get my letter? It's weird to write without knowing, but Mom says a letter to Kenya takes a while, and I should write once a week no matter what. That's OK, because I like writing.

I look at your picture on my cork board, and that helps. I wish I had eyes as big as yours. The picture I'm sending is from school, and those are never good, but my parents won't let me have a phone until I'm older, so I can't take a selfie. My hair is longer now, all the way down my back. Freddie Bigelow, who's in my class, calls me Blondie, but I don't answer. Mom says you probably don't have a laptop, and she wants me to practice my handwriting, anyway. Dad says this is Old School, but that's OK, he says, New School isn't always better. He's a librarian at the university, so he likes books. Mom works at the university, too, she teaches Environmental Studies, which is about pollution and stuff. Do you go to school? I just finished fifth grade, and I hate it. Why do they think I would want to know all the state capitals? And why is Freddie Bigelow so creepy? I know you wouldn't know, but it's a question I ask The Universe.

Your friend,
Harper

Dear Yez,

People think it doesn't get hot in Vermont, but let me tell you, it's hot now. And it's only June! My mom doesn't believe in air conditioning, she says fresh air is good for you, and we should experience all the seasons, but I can't sleep when it's so hot, I get all twisted up in the sheets, and I don't like the night noises, like crickets screeking and sirens on Pine Street. I can smell the Pijinowskys' garbage cans, but Mom says no I can't, that's just the smell of nature "doing its thing." I don't know how to spell

Pijinowsky. Nature can do its thing all it wants, but if we had AC I wouldn't have to smell it.

Did you see the moon last night? Do you get the same moon in Kenya? It was so big, it was brighter than the street lights. Dad says all the full moons have names, and this one is the Strawberry Moon. I sat up reading after Lights Out, and once in a while I looked out my window and saw that the moon had moved further West, which means it's moving away from you, too. But then it will go all the way around the Earth and you'll see it tomorrow before I do, which is weird, but that's what Mr. Terwilleger said in science class. That's the only class I miss. I'm not supposed to stay up so late, but if they didn't want me to read after Lights Out they shouldn't have given me the Itty-Bitty reading light.

I'm reading this book called *Anna and the French Kiss*, Addie gave it to me. The book is set in Paris, which is the most beautiful city in the world. That's what Mom says, and she lived there so she should know. Mom and Dad went to Paris together once, pre-Bean, as Dad says. I want to go someday, and climb the Eiffel Tower.

Mom is at the garden now, but she said I should stay here and write to you until Dad gets home. She spends a lot of time at the garden, which is still mostly just a dirty place in the park where they dug out the grass on a hill that was too steep for soccer but not long enough for sledding. She says it should have been planted in the spring, so the first crops can be ready this fall, but this is what happens when people drag their heels. Dad says it's what happens when you try to make people do things as a group. Mom organized everyone on our street, so we could grow peas and carrots and not have to buy them at Shaw's. Do you like peas? Neither do I. Carrots are OK with peanut butter. Sometimes Dad and I help with the digging and stuff, but mostly he says it's Mom's thing, which means he'd rather go for a walk with Sloppy Joe. Do you have a dog? Sloppy is a big black Lab with floppy ears and gray around his mouth, and he's the best. Dad says, "He's part wolfhound, just like me." Then he shouts "Mac Attack!" and he tackles Sloppy, and pins him to the living room floor, and beats one two three on the carpet, then stands and holds up his fist and shouts, "The winner! And still champeen!" Mom says "Not in the house!" Sloppy whines the whole time, which is what he does when he's happy.

Are you happy?

Your friend,
Harper

Dear Yez,

Why don't you write back? I asked Mom, and she said maybe you're busy. She said kids in Kenya have a lot of chores, they help with the farm, sometimes they don't even go to school. That would be so cool. It's OK if you're busy, I don't mind. I'm going to keep writing anyway.

What's Kenya like? If I had a phone, I could look it up. Dad says, "You *can* look it up!" and I look at him like, How?, and he points at the encyclopedia. And I say "Right, if I wanted to know about Kenya in like 1976!" He says, "The world doesn't change as much as you think, Bean." All my friends have their own phones. When they're surfing on the bus or the playground, I feel like an alien. I never remember to look Kenya up when we have computer lab at school, because they always make us do stuff like look up the capital of Indiana. Indianaoplis! Who cares?

When I walk to the mailbox, I always count my steps in French. Un deux trois quatre cinq six sept huit neuf dix. That's as high as I can go, so I start over and do it again. On the way back, sometimes I stop at Cumby's — don't tell Mom. They have the best AC. I look at magazines until the sweat on my neck gets dry. Do you know French? I know you know English, because Kenya used to belong to England, but maybe you have French in school, too? Common talley voo?

Votre ami,
Harper

Dear Yez,

This is completely unfair. I got grounded because Mom found some Skittles in my pocket, and she asked me where I got them, and I said Addie gave them to me, and then Mom called Addie's mom and told her I'm not allowed to have candy, and Addie's mom said OK, Addie won't give me any more. But Addie gets to have Skittles all the time, which is completely unfair. Mom says I shouldn't have accepted them. But Addie's my friend, it would be rude not to accept a gift, right? Next time I'm going to eat them all right away.

So now I'm not allowed to leave the house by

myself, which is stupid because it's summer and the park is only like three houses away, that's where I like to meet with Addie. I can go higher on the swings than anybody. I'm still allowed to walk to the mailbox, because writing to you = A Good Thing. But Mom checks her watch when I leave the house, so I don't dilly-dally.

The sheet I got about you says you have two brothers and three sisters, which is crazy. What's that like? Sometimes I wish I had siblings, because I wouldn't have Mom watching me all the time. No matter what I do, there's Mom, like a hawk, swoop swoop. Dad doesn't swoop, but he watches me, too, all the time. He says, "it's just because we love you, Bean." But sometimes I wish I was invisible, you know?

BTW, Dad calls me Bean, or sometimes Sprout, they're both short for Beansprout, because I'm so tall. And sometimes he calls me Daddy's Little Monster.

Are you more like your mother or your father? This is a question Addie asked me, and I said I don't know, but she said I had to know, it's part of who I am. She says she's more like her mom, that's where she gets her dimples. I think she's too full of herself, but her dimples are PDC, which is Pretty Darn Cute. She says she's not like her father, he has a beard, and he smells like deodorant, because he has BO, and who would want that? I said let me think about it, and so I'm thinking. Here's what my parents are like.

Mom is skinny like me, and I'm almost as tall as her already, she says she can't stand it. Addie asked what makes her happy? It's hard to say. With Dad, you know it's when he's out on the deck with Sloppy, drinking a beer and listening to the Red Sox—only he gets so upset when they lose, I don't know if that's really happy anymore. But I know he's happy on Saturday morning when he sleeps in and then he comes out in his old bathrobe that Mom hates. He makes coffee and sings this song about java, a cup a cup a cup a cup a cup, then he puts an English muffin in the toaster and pours honey all over his plate, so he can sop it up. He says honey is God's food, it makes him happy as a hedgehog. And he's also happy when he's doing stuff around the house, like building the deck or painting my room, he whistles like a madman. Sometimes he plays guitar and sings, and he's not very good, but he has such a good time, that makes it good, you know? He sings this song called "The Lament of the Mosstrooper," which goes "So we'll go no more a rovin', no more a rovin', we'll go no more a rovin' by the light of the moon," and he builds up to this big moment that goes "Alack the day!" and it's supposed to be sad, that's what alack means, but it just makes him so happy to sing it. Later, he walks around the house singing Alack the day! all day long.

And Mom? I want to say it's when she's in the garden, because it's so important to her, but when she's there all she does is find stones and slugs and jimson weed, and I wouldn't call that happy. But maybe it's happy in its own way. On Sunday morning, when Dad is still in bed, she puts on the classical station, and they play "early music," and she always says this doesn't mean the time of day. I get it, Mom. Dad calls it "Lutes and Flutes." That's when she cleans the house "from stem to stern." It sounds crazy, but I think that's when she's happy. When Dad comes in, we give her a hard time about it. I say, "Why do we have to clean all the time? It'll just get dirty again!"

Dad gives me a thumbs up that he thinks Mom won't see, because she's on her hands and knees with a scrub-bucket.

She says, "'We'? I don't see *you* with a broom, Princess Pitty-Pat! And I saw that, Mac McKenzie!"

Dad likes to let dishes pile up in the sink and then "rally" to wash them with some good dishwashing music, like his Rolling Stones mix. He says, "In Europe, the queens and kings had dozens of castles, so when one castle got dirty they could just move to another one."

I say, "I'm moving to Europe!"

Mom is scraping with her thumbnail at an invisible spot on the floor, and she says, "You can't clean with a filthy sponge."

I think I'm more like Dad, but I know Addie thinks the right answer would be Mom, so I said, "I'm more like Sloppy Joe!" Addie said this is a non-answer, but too bad for her.

Three pages! Time for dinner.

Your friend,

Harper

Dear Yez,

Do boys chase you? Freddie Bigelow used to chase me around during recess like it was his job. And then he just stopped. Dad says it's because I got my "growth spurt," and boys are scared by tall girls. Freddie has big ears and a bowl haircut, and he's really good at kickball, big woop. Nobody's faster than I am. Addie says if he chases her she's going to let him catch her, because she thinks he's cute, but seriously, what would he do then? I don't even want to know. Now that it's summer, maybe he's chasing people at the park, but I wouldn't know, would I, because I'm G-R-O-U-N-D-E-D. I asked Dad how long, and he said "Until your mother says." Which is totally bogus. Prisoners get sentences, right? I could be grounded for life!

The moon is waxing again, that means it's getting bigger, I don't know what it has to do with wax. Dad says the full moon next week will be the Buck Moon, which has to do with hunting, so he's all over it. He says it goes west because it's headed for a dip in Lake Champlain, to cool off. I don't think Mr. Terwilleger would agree, but it's summer, so I can't ask him.

BTW, Dad doesn't really go hunting. I mean, he goes, and he takes a gun and all, but he never shoots anything. He says, "Don't tell your mom," but I can tell you. He just likes being out in the woods. He says, "I go hunting, I just don't go catching."

What's your greatest fear? This is another question from Addie, who has to come over to our house, because I got extra-grounded, and I'm still not allowed to go to the park. I'll tell you about that in a minute. We sit on the front porch and drink lemonade and talk. I wish we could sit on the roof of the porch, which I can get to by climbing out my window, but I'm not allowed. Addie makes up these Life Questions. Her mom is a psychiatrist. She says her biggest fear is spiders, because they're the creepiest things, and wouldn't it be awful to get stuck in a web, just waiting to be eaten. I said I didn't know what mine was, and then I changed the subject to Freddie B., and that was fine with her.

But I can tell you. My worst fear is that I'll become my mother. I got grounded longer because she found more candy in my room, and she asked me where it came from, and I started to say something about Addie again, but then I thought no, she'll take Addie away from me, so I said I didn't know, and she said it didn't just drop out of the sky, and I looked up at the ceiling, which just made her madder, and she said I was grounded until I could start telling the truth.

Afterward, I went into the upstairs bathroom and locked the door, and I lay down in the empty bathtub. That's the coolest place in the house. And I said to myself, I am never going to have children, because I would be just like her.

Harper

Dear Yez,

It's still hot. Today Addie didn't want to come over here and sit with me in the sweatbox, because she has AC at home. The only time it gets cool is at night. It's late now, with the fan in the window and the Itty-Bitty light clamped to my desk.

Today Dad let me watch him shave, he knows I like it. He lathers up with the big schwaaa sound from the can, then he says, "Here we go. Cheek the Left." And he clears his left cheek with a few swipes of the blade, rinses the razor, and says, "Cheek the Right." Clears it. Then he says, "Burnsides." He says sideburns are named after a Union general from the Civil War, Somebody Burnside, who had big ones. Men are strange. Then he goes, "The Underchin," and he scrapes off all the foam there. He says, "One must be very careful here, because of that very precious item, the Adding's Apple." That's how he says it, he knows it's wrong. Then he says, "A big Adding's Apple is a sign of high intelligence."

I feel my throat. "But I don't have one!"

He gives me the Gotcha look. He is such a goombah. But he knows it.

He keeps looking at me in the bathroom mirror, and he says, "Sprout, you know your mother loves you, right?"

What could I say? He still had scraps of foam on his face. "Yeah."

He held my eyes. "Good." Then he ducked his head down to splash off the last bits of foam. When he came up and toweled off, he said, "I look like a new man!" He always says that.

I said what I always say, which is "We can always hope."

"Burn!" he said, and went off to get dressed for work.

Maybe it's cool enough to sleep now.

Harper

Dear Yez,

Sloppy ran away! Can you believe it? It's terrible!

Dad was walking him in the woods at Red Rocks, a few miles from here, and Sloppy got off his leash, which probably means Dad let him off the leash, but he knows Mom doesn't like that—and Sloppy started chasing a squirrel, and Dad called and called until after dark, but he never came back! Dad came home late, and I was already in bed, but I wasn't asleep, and I noticed that I couldn't hear Sloppy's tags jingling, or Dad talking to him, so I got up and went to the kitchen, and Dad told me all about it. He looked so miserable. Alack the day!

I asked if Sloppy could find his way home, and Dad said definitely, dogs have such powerful noses that they can sniff out their owners from miles away. They follow the "scent stream," and it leads them right home.

So the next day, that is today, I took four of my T-shirts, and I rubbed them against me and put one of them on each corner of our yard. Mom didn't want my shirts out in the grass, but she could tell I was upset, so she didn't stop me. Now we wait.

Your friend,
Harper

Dear Yez,

Sloppy didn't come home, so you know what I did? I cut off my hair! Not all of it, but a lot, it was getting too long anyway. I thought maybe he couldn't smell my T-shirts because they had been washed too much, but what if I put my hair out there? When he saw me, Dad raised an eyebrow, but he just said, "Summer cut, Bean?" Of course, Mom freaked, but what's she going to do? I'm already grounded. And why can't I cut my hair if I want? It's my hair! I just want Sloppy to come home! But then the next day it rained really hard, and when I went out to check afterwards a lot of the hair had been washed away, it was just these little dirty yellow clumps. They smelled like mud. What are we going to do?

Harper

Dear Yez,

What's the worst thing you ever did? For the longest time I thought the worst was stealing stuff from Cumby's. Not much, you know, just candy bars, little things I could slip in my pocket. I wasn't allowed to buy it, so what was I supposed to do? Plus, it was a game, like what could I get away with?

Well, I snuck out. I was still grounded, and I was sick of it. And Addie said we should go to the skate park by the lake, because Freddie was going to be there. And I thought, gross, I don't need that dude. But this was the first thing Addie had asked me to do in ages, and I didn't want to say no. I didn't tell her I was still grounded. It was Saturday morning, and Mom was busy in her office, and Dad wasn't up yet. I just snuck out, and left my door closed like I was sleeping in. I met Addie at the bus stop on Pine Street, and we rode the bus downtown, the skate park is a short walk from there. We both have bus passes for getting to school. All the time, I was buzzing, you know how your head gets when you're excited? Only I didn't want to see Freddie.

So when we arrived downtown and got off the

bus, the first thing we saw was this guy lying on the ground in front of the cathedral. I've never been inside, because "that's not our club," as Dad says, but outside they have this little park full of locust trees, Mom says it's a great example of an urban green space, but the buses park right next to it, so it's always full of noise and fumes. Still, sometimes people sleep there in the shade of those trees. So there was this guy, lying next to a bicycle, and we couldn't see his face because he was facing the other way, but we could see his butt crack! His shirt had pulled out of his pants, you know? It was gross. But Addie pointed, and we giggled, and then Addie looked at me with wide eyes, which is The Dare Look. And I gave it back to her. So she pulled out a pencil, and pointed at the man in the grass. And I laughed, and my look said No way, Rozay! But I took the pencil.

I walked over there, under the shade of those trees, and I went up to the guy. He was snoring really loud, I probably could have been banging on a drum, but I went on my tiptoes until I was right next to him. I looked back at Addie, who was watching me all the way. Then I took the pencil, and as quick as I could, I stuck it in his butt crack! Don't worry, I used the eraser end. He snorted, but he didn't wake up. So I got out of there, running this time. And that's the worst thing I ever did. So far. It was fun, though.

Addie was laughing like mad, but then she wanted to go on down to the skate park, and I said no, I needed to get home. I don't think she really cared, she just wanted to go make goo-goo eyes at

Freddie Bigelow on his board. So I got on the next bus, and I snuck in the back door of the house. Mom was still in her office, and Dad was still asleep, so you could say nothing happened at all.

Your friend,

Harper

Dear Yez,

Sloppy Joe hasn't come back. Dad tried to explain it to me. Sometimes, he said, dogs just need to wander. They're animals, after all, they weren't meant to be cooped up in a house, they get itchy. I think Dad really believes this, but I don't know, maybe he's just trying to make me feel better. Addie said that when their dog didn't come home it was because he got hit by a car, and the police didn't report it to them for over a week. But it's been three weeks since Sloppy ran off, wouldn't they have found him by now?

Last night, when he tucked me in, Dad said another thing. He usually reads me a story, but sometimes he makes things up. Or I don't know, maybe they're true. This time it sounded true, because it was so strange, that's how you know. He told me about this kind of sea turtle that lives on an island off the coast of Georgia. I think it's called Dafuskey, I don't know how to spell it. Anyway, he said the mother turtle lays her eggs in the sand near the shore, then she takes off. She doesn't need to keep them warm, because they're cold-blooded. Weeks later, they hatch. And the little sea turtles come out, and they stretch, and they sniff the air, and they see the moon. They always follow the moon.

I asked what if it's cloudy, and he said they wait until it's clear. So they follow the moon, which is rising over the ocean. And suddenly they're in the water, and they're swimming.

And they swim for miles and miles—like hundreds of miles, because they have to get to this special place out in the ocean called the Sargasso Sea. They settle on some islands there. But Dad said a lot of them don't make it. He said only one in a thousand makes landfall. I never heard that word before, but I could tell what he meant.

And then that one turtle, the one in a thousand, she grows up there, on that island in the Sargasso Sea. And years later, when she's ready, she swims back to Dafuskey, and she lays her own eggs, and the whole thing starts over again.

I think the story was really about Sloppy. I don't know if he's itching or swimming or running in the woods, but I think he's out there.

Good night, Yez.

Harper Harper Harper
Harper Harper

Dear Yez,

Today Mom took me to a rally for protecting a wetland down by the lake. I'm still grounded, but she had this rally, and she wasn't going to leave me home alone. It seems kind of crazy to shout about a wetland, I mean, isn't land supposed to be dry? The lake was just fifty yards away, if you wanted to be wet. But Mom says wetlands are important places for certain plants and animals to live, and the city is planning to clear this one so they can put in a parking lot for the sailing center, and she says people should walk or take the bus, there are too many cars on the waterfront already.

So we took the bus, and we marched and shouted for a while, and I kept hearing this strange noise in the background, but I couldn't tell what it was until we took a break for lunch. Mom and I sat on a bench by the bikepath and I looked over to the right, and there was the skatepark! It was packed with kids. One of the boarders was this tall guy in a black T-shirt who was really good. He took all those hills and dips and double pipes super fast, and he never fell once. I wish I could be good at something like that.

When we walked back to the bus stop, I saw these big white words painted on the bikepath, like this:

AHEAD

STOP

and

RIGHT

KEEP

I asked Mom why they were upside down, and she said they were for cyclists and runners who are going fast, so they can read the words from the bottom. The strangest one said

XING

PED

Which sounds like the name of a panda at the zoo. Mom said it was "pedestrian crossing," but I like the panda idea better.

FRIEND

YOUR,

Harper

Dear Yez,

Do you even exist? I think Mom and Dad have given up hope; they don't ask anymore if I've heard from you. But I know you're out there. I picture you laughing, like in the picture they sent. One of your sisters just cracked a joke, or no, you just told *them* about this crazy American girl with the bright red tongue and the packages of Skittles tucked in her armpits. Did I tell you about that? How else am I going to sneak them into the house?

And then and then and then and then and then—can you stand the suspense? Sloppy came home! We were sitting out in the back yard one night with Evie and Leah from across the street, they were talking about their gall bladders and I was trying to catch fireflies and put them in a jar. Suddenly I heard this jingling sound, and there he was, loping into the yard like the King of Siam. Dad raced over to him, but I got there first, because nobody's faster than I am. I hugged him hard. He was so skinny! And man did he stink. Mom said he should get a bath right away. I said that would just make him run away again, but she said he wasn't going in the house without a bath. So Dad filled the wading pool with the hose, and sprayed all of us while he was at it, and he threw bubble bath in, until there were gazillions of bubbles shining in the backyard floodlight. And then he tossed Sloppy in, and I jumped in too, I was just wearing shorts and a T-shirt. Sloppy whined like crazy. And then Mom made me take a real bath before going to bed.

I'm glad he's back, of course. I love Sloppy, he's still the best. But I'll never trust him again.

Your friend,

Harper

Dear Yez,

I'm down to my last stamp and envelope. You know what that means. It feels like Sunday afternoon, my unfavorite day, when you can't enjoy the time because Monday is hanging over you. The burning bush in our front yard has started going red on top. Mom says she can't stand it. She gets itchy about going back to school, she's always behind schedule, there aren't enough days left, but you can tell she's really pumped, it's what she does. Dad, he just gets sad. Baseball season has almost disappeared, and it won't be back till April.

I got ungrounded — just in time for school, yippee.

It's hot again, as if it doesn't know that summer's gone. Mom says enough already. Everybody's grouchy.

Did you see the moon last night? Or maybe you'll see last night's moon tonight? Dad says it's the Sturgeon Moon. I asked him how to spell it. It's a kind of fish, so when it goes to dunk itself in the cool water of the lake, it can just go on swimming. Last night I climbed out on the porch roof to watch it. Dad had already put me to bed, but I didn't want to sleep. I don't care if they ground me again, now that I have to be stuck in school anyway.

I watched until it sank behind the trees across the street — and then I decided to follow it. The upstairs hall was dark. I put on shorts and sneakers, then I slipped downstairs, out the front door, and down the street. It was so late, so quiet, my sneakers slapped the sidewalk. I passed Cumby's, lit up bright like always. Just think of all those Skittles on the shelves. But I was following the moon.

It led me to the lake, to this little beach Dad showed me once. You take this secret path at the end of a dead-end street, and you duck under some trees, and suddenly you come out on this tiny triangle of sand. It's about big enough for three people, standing up. And some beer cans. I just wanted to see the fish moon hit the water.

Well, it didn't. I mean, probably it did, but I couldn't tell, because in the last ten minutes a bank of clouds came up, and the moon disappeared. But I imagined the rest.

Bye, Yez. I'll miss you.

Harper

TRANSIENT

It is 25 below zero, and all the world is white. The only sound, besides his own steady breathing, is the *shoos shoos shoos* of his skis sliding uphill. Day 19, and he feels strong. With a leather harness strapped around his waist, he pulls the three-hundred-pound sled that carries his tent, his tools, his one change of clothing, and all the food he needs for this journey. His thighs hum with the effort of skiing uphill — and this, he thinks, is what thighs are for. Trekking as much as sixteen hours a day, he burns so many calories that he must stop often to eat — beef jerky, duck jerky, turkey jerky. When he returns to England, Cecily will serve him heaps of fresh fruit and vegetables, custard and cream. For now, he is counting on the creatures that metabolized all those nutrients for him. Watching him pack, just three weeks ago, his eleven-year-old daughter called it "The Jerky Expedition." He smiled and said, "Har-har."

Mac McKenzie entertained this fantasy while sitting

at the reference desk on a slow Tuesday afternoon. His wife's name was not Cecily but Ruth. She thought those books about polar expeditions were a crazy waste of time. Mac had never been to England, much less to Antarctica. Harper, his real-life daughter, called it Anarchica. She did not watch him pack, because in fact he did not pack; he never went anywhere. Well, soon he would make his November hunting trip with Hooley and Skiff, but that didn't count; they wouldn't even leave Vermont.

"Heads up, Mac," said Silverman from the next desk. "It's her again." Silverman was the other reference librarian on duty weekday afternoons. He was a sinewy little guy in jeans and a denim shirt, with wire-rimmed glasses and a graying ponytail. He looked like he might have played soccer in college — if they had soccer back then.

The "her" in question was a platinum-blond woman bearing down on the reference desk. Jocelyn Winters was Chair of the Political Science department — Ruth's department. It wouldn't be her department much longer, if the Faculty Assembly approved her proposal for a new major in Environmental Studies, which she would chair. At the meeting to discuss the proposal, Winters argued that it was impractical, expensive, and "unscholarly." Mac always skipped these meetings, but he heard all about it from his exasperated wife, and also from Silverman, who agitated side by side with Ruth. When Jocelyn Winters approached the reference desk — a square of counters in the middle of the open-plan ground floor — Silverman disappeared.

"This morning in Public Policy," she said with no pre-lude but an icy blue glare, "a student started spouting some fire-breathing stuff about direct action. When I said it was nonsense, he said, 'But you put it on reserve reading!' I said I most certainly did not. And yet when I checked the reserve list online, there it was. How could this happen?"

A slender woman in a charcoal sweater set, Winters was in her early forties—just a few years older than Mac and Ruth. She knew very well who Mac was—they had met at various departmental gatherings, and he had helped her set up the reserve list this fall—but she was too furious now for niceties. Mac didn't mind; in fact, he got a kick out of watching academics get all worked up over their precious teacups. When Winters flashed those imperious eyes at him, he slid straight to extra polite.

"I don't know how this could have happened, Professor." He studied the computer monitor that stood between them, and made a note on a pad of paper beside it. "I'll notify my colleague who manages the online reserve."

"Please do," she snapped. "This is ridiculous. It's one thing to have students citing activist folderol in class—it happens all the time, thanks to some of my colleagues—but I won't have them believing that I actually assigned it." She tossed her glossy coif back and walked away.

Mac turned to Silverman, just now emerging from his keyhole desk. "What's the deal?" he asked.

"I don't like that woman," Silverman said.

"But you'll fix it?"

"Yeah." He tucked Mac's scribbled note into a folder on his desk. "But right now I've got to get downtown." He had been jetting away from work every afternoon to take part in the Occupy Burlington demonstration in City Hall Park. Ruth had often been there, too, taking Harper along after school. Jocelyn Winters's reserve reading list would have to wait.

Day 26. Conditions serene. His breath smokes in the blue air. He covered eighteen nautical miles today—a good day, quiet, nothing to see but ice and sky. He knows this weather won't last. If he is going to reach the Pole by New Year's Day, he must make good time while he can. He has planned carefully, beginning his trek in October, the first days of the Polar summer, when the temperature can climb as high as twenty degrees Fahrenheit. Still, he knows that storms can arise anytime.

Antarctica is the coldest place on earth. And also the driest: it receives so little rainfall that technically it qualifies as a desert. With an average altitude over 8,000 feet, it is the highest of the continents. He has done his research; it doesn't make him any warmer. Even on a calm day, the air singes his lungs.

But stranger than the cold is the perpetual daylight. The sun rose in September, before he arrived, and it will not set until March. At the end of a day—he can hardly call it night—there is just a slight dimming in the sky, azure paling to lavender. As he makes camp, pounding tent stakes into the ice, he thinks of Cecily back home with their daughter. On long summer evenings, the Bean always chafed at being put to bed before dark.

In the half-light of his tent, he studies the map like a Talmudic scholar. It's the best map he could get, based on Scott's 1900 expedition, just eleven years ago. Still, most of it is blank. What else could it be? With a frost-bitten finger he traces the long slope he has been climbing – the Titan Dome. It rises from the Weddell Sea across almost half the continent, which is the size of Europe. Near the top, nine thousand feet above sea level, his finger stops at a single dot: the Pole. The top of his climb, but the bottom of the world, where all the lines of longitude converge, and the earth no longer spins.

"It's happened again," she said.

It was two days later, and Jocelyn Winters was back at the counter. Her eyes seemed even bluer. Silverman had disappeared again. The eyes bored in on Mac.

"Same class," she said, "but a different student this time. She started reciting statistics about the 'one per cent' – how much wealth they possess, how much they consume, how little is left for 'ordinary people,' and blah blah blah – and I said, 'What does that have to do with Obama's position on the inheritance tax?' She said, 'It's all connected!' and I said, 'Who says that?' and she said, 'Noam Chomsky! It was on our reading for today!'"

Winters paused for effect. "I did *not* put that on my reading list. But then I checked the list online, and lo and behold: Noam Chomsky, in all his leftist glory. If I wanted to teach a course on do-gooding radicalism, I'd call it 'Power to the People' and serve Peace Pops every day." She pulled herself up taller over Mac's computer station. "What's going on here?"

"I'm terribly sorry, Professor. I don't know how this keeps happening. I definitely notified our computer guy. There seems to be a bug in the system." Once again, he made a note on a slip of paper.

"Well, de-bug it! I can't have these mixed messages mucking up my course!" Again, a flip of the platinum hair, and she stalked away.

Silverman emerged from the storage cabinet where he had been kneeling, as if intently looking for something. "I do not like that woman," he said.

"But you'll fix it?" Mac said.

"Yeah." He smiled. "It's a complicated system. But you know what? I don't think she really *wants* it fixed."

"What do you mean? Didn't you hear her?"

"I think she's sweet on you, man."

Mac shook his head. "What? She's ready to tear me a new one."

"Oh, she talks tough. But you know, people express affection in surprising ways."

"I think you're nuts. Let's just fix the problem."

"I'm on it, never fear." Silverman slipped the piece of paper in his folder. Then he took off for Occupy again. He said the crowd was growing. There were some fifty people camped out in City Hall Park, with speeches and demonstrations every day. He didn't want to miss the action.

In his tent after another good day of trekking, he chews on some jerky. Beef, or mutton? No matter. Each time he takes a hunk of it from the sled, he thinks twice. Does he really need this? There is only so much food, and so far to go. Never before has he been so aware of transforming the world into energy. Every bite translates into more miles covered. He chews slowly. Then he cleans his teeth with a cup of snow melted over the fire, using the boar-bristle brush Cecily gave him the night before he left. "Hygiene!" she said. "You never know who you'll meet down there."

He smiled. He knew what was coming.

"And when you return, there's your audience with the Queen!"

Their little joke. Just because he kept that portrait of Alexandra in his study.

It must be hard for Cecily now, to be on her own with the Bean. But surely it will be best for all three of them. He knows his daughter must miss him fiercely — and her dependence on him was part of why he had to go. How could an eleven-year-old fathom that? He can only hope that someday she will understand. He stretches out in his quilted sack, pulls his sleeping mask on, and the world dissolves.

The next day, Silverman was less chipper than usual. "It's Willow," he said. "And this new boyfriend."

They were on their lunch break, in the library's basement

snack room. Mac loved the vending machines — Cheez-Doodles, sugary granola bars, cans of Dr. Pepper. Ruth would definitely frown on such items at home. She wanted only healthy foods for Harper. Mac knew she was right, but, well, sometimes he backslid.

Willow was Silverman's twenty-five-year-old daughter. After the divorce, ten years back, he had raised her on his own, because his ex, he said, was a certifiable nutbird. Willow had had a bumpy path, but in recent years she'd been steady, waiting tables at the Rotisserie out on Williston Road. Just until she found something better, Silverman said.

Mac asked, "What's wrong with the boyfriend?"

"He's a Nazi! Last night, when I mentioned Occupy, he said it was just a bunch of pampered kids pretending to be homeless. I almost choked on my lasagna."

Mac laughed, but he knew this was serious, too. Silverman went on. "I try to be an understanding parent. I know it's tough for Willow without a mother. When she got in trouble in grade school, I always took her side. When she got into drugs, I didn't freak out; I mean, I've been known to ingest the occasional controlled substance myself." He grinned a spiky grin. "When she dropped out of high school, I said OK, the educational system is messed up, it's not for everybody. Have I not been understanding?"

"Exceedingly."

"But a boyfriend who loves Sarah Palin? This is a bridge too far."

"I hear you, man." Whatever Mac said to Silverman sounded better punctuated by "man."

Silverman looked up from his sandwich. "Hey, maybe you could talk to her?"

"Oh, I don't think so. What would I say?"

"Maybe you could get a sense of how serious this is. She's always liked you; maybe she'll open up. If I'm going to have a right-wing son-in-law, I might just have to kill myself." He stuffed the rest of his sandwich into his backpack. "Right now, though, I gotta run."

On Day 35, he finds a penguin skull embedded in the ice. He's no paleontologist: he can't tell how old it is. But he wonders: where are the other bones? Where are the other penguins?

His beard is almost always crusted with ice, thanks to breath condensing inside the balaclava. He did not anticipate this. But it amuses him, in the dim tent at night, when he gazes at his reflection in the little mirror of his kit: the snowy whiskers show him a glimpse of an older self.

Sometimes, as he skis, he finds himself chanting. "Alone, alone, all all alone, alone on a wide wide sea." He sees the words projected on a white screen in his mind, like the big screen at the Electric Cinema in Portobello Road. He always wanted to be a poet. Miss Neville told him in sixth form that his poems were "nice." He could tell she was being kind.

Soon after noon on Friday, Mac felt a presence near the reference desk, and he knew without looking up: it was Jocelyn Winters again. Indeed, she was looming over his station.

He said, "Don't tell me it's happened again."

She smiled. "No, I checked the list this morning online, and it looks like you've been quite efficient." She looked beyond him, around the desk. Silverman was already off to City Hall Park. No students were about; the weekend was beginning. "I have something else in mind."

"What can I do for you?"

"I'd rather not talk about it here. It's not library business."

"I see."

"Today after work," she said. "Three thirty? You name the place. Somewhere off campus."

He was nodding like an idiot. He didn't see how he could say no. He said, "How about the Rotisserie?"

On Day 41, the wind sweeps him off his feet. Tangled in the harness, he struggles to get back on his skis. He knows the great danger that lurks in the ice: crevasses large enough to swallow a man, who would never be heard from again. When the wind whips, ice crystals swirl around him like drifts of ash, and visibility drops to zero. It's like being trapped inside a Ping-Pong ball. He simply has to stop.

Fighting the gale, he stakes his sled into the ice. Wouldn't he feel a right fool if the wind blew his precious supplies away? Then he pitches his tent and hunkers down in his sleeping bag, where he lies awake for hours, listening to the wind. He frets at this loss of time. It is now mid-December, and he is intent on making the Pole by New Year's Day. But the storm may have other things in mind.

Twice, the wind seems to abate enough for travel, so he strikes his tent and starts on his way. Twice, he is knocked off his skis within the hour. He can see nothing but the ice below his feet. Unable to guess where the sun is in the sky, he can't be sure that he isn't just making big circles, burning useless calories. He pictures himself from above, and sees great cursive loops on the snow, nonsense words that will be erased by the wind within minutes. *Runcible, ranunculus, randoon.* He makes camp again, and seethes before a fire. His food will last only so long.

For the first time, here it is: fear.

Mac had always liked The Rotisserie. It was like the bars of his bachelor days — dark and simple and unapologetically devoted to alcohol and sports. It was far enough from campus that students seldom hung out there, even for reverse chic. His old green pickup didn't seem out of place in the parking lot. Walking into this dark room with its aroma of lager and peanuts and its perpetual soundtrack of classic rock, you could think it was 1975.

He was twenty minutes early. There was nobody in the booths or at the bar, where little hanging lanterns cast pools of light. SportsCenter was recycling highlights of last week's NFL action. His beloved baseball couldn't get screen time even during the World Series. There by the register, studying her phone, was Willow.

What a relief it must be to her that her name did not turn out to be ironic. Tall and thin, with dark blond hair in a simple shoulder-length cut, she seemed well rooted in the world. Although Mac had known her since she was small, when her mother was still around, he hadn't seen much of her in recent years. He heard about her adventures from Silverman, who took as much pride in each step as if she was completing a Ph.D. in neurophysics. When she looked up, a smile lit her face.

"Mr. Mac! What brings you to the Rot?"

He smiled, too. "Do they still call it that?"

She looked around with apparent pleasure. Stools with red faux-leather seats, bowling trophies over the bar, pictures of Little League teams by the bathrooms. "What else could you call this place?"

He told her he was meeting someone, and they'd probably want a booth—but for now he lingered at the bar. He didn't know what Jocelyn Winters would be drinking, but it was Friday afternoon at the Rot, and he was going to have a Narragansett.

"I hear you're working on your G.E.D.," he said.

"Yeah," she said as she set a stein before him. "It seemed like time, you know?"

"Good for you. We all have to do these things at our own pace. Sometimes I think I rushed everything too much."

She nodded, but didn't inquire about particulars.

"I hear there's a new boyfriend, too?"

"Oh, that's not so new. That's been, like, six months now."

"So should I be getting my suit cleaned for the wedding?"

"Hey, my wedding will be worth a new suit!" She laughed, a lovely little musical cascade. "No, we're not tying any knots. Not yet. But yeah," she added, looking out the window to the traffic on Williston Road. "It's good."

"What's his name?"

"Kyle."

"Your father says he's uh, somewhat conservative."

"Yeah, well, everyone looks somewhat conservative to my father." She laughed. "OK, maybe not your wife. She and Dad are birds of a feather. But you know, maybe politics aren't everything? Don't tell Dad I said that. The thing is, Kyle is nice to me. I like him. The sex is good, you know?" She laughed again. "So how *is* your wife?" Then she caught herself. "I don't mean how's the sex life. I mean, how *is* she? I heard she had a cancer scare."

"Yeah, but she's OK now. Stable. More committed to her work than ever. I hardly ever see her these days. As soon as she finishes on campus, she heads off to City Hall Park for Occupy."

"I thought her thing was the environment."

"It is. Don't get her started on how Occupy is really an environmental issue."

Willow nodded. "Well, everything is connected, right?"

"I guess."

"Kyle was at Occupy the other day."

"He was? But—"

"I know, he's not the Occupy type. But he's fascinated by the whole thing, you know? He's just observing. And probably heckling a little, you need some hecklers, right? Then you know you're doing something right." She leaned toward Mac, hands on the bar. "He says they chant, 'We Are The Ninety-Nine Per Cent!'—kind of an awkward chant, if you ask me—and he calls back, 'Your Math Is Flawed!' Weird, I know—but he's like that. He says the whole Ninety-Nine Per Cent thing is a crock, it's more like fifty-fifty. Fifty per cent who think some people make too much money, and fifty per cent who wish they could *be* one of those people."

"But if it's fifty-fifty, then there's no one per cent. Unless my math is flawed."

"Exactly! He says it's all hype."

"Well, there's no shortage of *that* going around."

"I know, right?" She gestured to his empty glass. "Get you another?"

He knew he shouldn't. But Jocelyn Winters was fifteen minutes late now. Probably she was one of those academics who are too busy to be on time for anything. Maybe she wasn't going to show at all. Maybe she had texted him about it. But it would feel wrong to check his phone. Way too millennial for the Rot.

Willow said, "Come on, it's on the house!"

"Can you do that?"

She looked around the empty bar. "Do you see any-body watching?"

"Well, in that case—"

She took his glass and pulled the tap, then looked past him to the door. "This must be your date."

Before Mac could say "Oh, it's not a date," Jocelyn Winters had reached the bar in a flurry of scarves, flutter-ing over her Burberry. She had probably been eager for the cold weather to arrive, bringing more opportunities for layering.

She said, "Can we get a booth?".

Willow swept a be-my-guest arm across the room, and Jocelyn went straight for the darkest corner. "I'll have a Manhattan," she said, as she took off her coat. "Straight up. Crown Royal, if you've got it." Willow nodded, as if to say, Of course we have it. We're the freakin' Rot!

"So," Jocelyn said, as soon as she sat down, "This is about Ruth and Occupy." OK, Mac thought, nice to see you, too. "It would really be best if she didn't spend so much time there."

Mac paused, then asked, "Has her teaching suffered?"

"Not that I know of, no."

"Is she failing to attend to some other university duties? Committees, advising, all that stuff?"

"No, but—"

"Then I don't see how it's your business what she does with her own time."

Willow brought the Manhattan, saw that Mac's second beer was fine, and left them alone. Several Friday afternoon customers came in and took a booth near the door.

Jocelyn took a sip, winced — did that mean good or bad? — and spoke again.

"The thing is, it's not exactly her own time. As a professor, she's a very public figure. City Hall Park is a very public place. She has classes full of students who take note of her behavior."

"She's quite aware of that. And she's glad to have them see how committed she is to the issues."

Another sip, another wince. "But I'm not glad. It's unprofessional, unscholarly, unwise. She can't remain objective if she's on a picket line. Her new program might get more support if she's more circumspect."

Mac smiled. Circumspection had never been his wife's forte. "Have you spoken to her directly?"

"She won't listen to me."

"And you think that, even if I *were* willing to make this suggestion, she'd listen to me?"

"I thought you might be concerned." Another sip. "I understand she's been bringing your daughter along."

How did she know? He didn't ask. "So?"

"It's dangerous! This isn't just a little campus rally! You know what that park is like. Yes, some of the protesters are politely camped in their yurts, powering their laptops by pedaling bikes connected to generators. How lovely for them. And in the next tent there's a couple of homeless guys, strung out on who knows what, just there for the free pizza that someone has started distributing every day. Is that a good environment for your daughter?"

Mac took a sip of his own. "I trust my wife's judgment," he said. "Thank you for your concern."

Winters gave him a long look, then stood and gathered her coat from the back of the booth. "Just think about it," she said. And she stalked off into the early November evening, scarves fluttering like banners behind her.

Mac exhaled. When Willow came over, he paid for Winters's pricey drink. He wished he could stay to chat, but the happy hour crowd was growing, and Willow had her hands full. It was time to get home, anyway, and get dinner started. Maybe Harper and Ruth would bring pizza home from the park.

On the evening of Day 41, he pulls out the flask of whiskey he was saving for a celebratory drink at the Pole. It shoots through his veins, warming him more than anything has done since the journey began. He tells himself this is just a pressure valve; a trekker needs to blow off steam. He downs another dram. Then he finds among his stores a packet of biscuits the Bean insisted he bring. He downs that, too. The sugar is so good.

Deciding to top this treat with a savory morsel, he digs out a hunk of jerky, and with the first bite he breaks a front tooth. It must have been rotten, awaiting its moment like a shelf of glacial ice when it calves.

The pain is immense and ridiculous. It is worse than his blistered feet, worse than his frostbitten fingers. Those, after all, are normal consequences of such a trek, predictable, explicable. This, though, this is just stupid.

He should not have had that drink. He should not have opened those biscuits. If he were back home, Cecily would make him tea. Dr. Speliotis would give him morphine. The Sprout would joke about his monstrous gap-toothed visage. In the little shaving mirror, he makes a hideous grin. The only thing for it is to finish off the flask.

"What a Bitch Queen!" Silverman exclaimed the following Monday. "It's good you shut her down, man." He may have heard Mac's account of the Rotisserie conversation in a slightly heroic register. He was glad to know that Willow's wedding was not imminent. Now he could focus on the texts he was getting from his comrades in the park.

There had been some scuffles over the weekend—something to do with a picket line at Citizens Bank, where Saturday customers weren't happy to be jeered for doing business with a bank owned by a corporation that received a "too big to fail" bailout. "Too bad if they can't take a little guff," said Silverman. "That's the cost of complicity." He stood at the reference desk to help a student, bouncing on the balls of his feet.

Winters did not come by again. Mac had said nothing to Ruth about their meeting at the Rotisserie. The attempt to intervene would just stiffen Ruth's resolve, which was stiff enough already. Every morning on NPR, Mac heard the latest from Zuccotti Park in New York—hundreds arrested, crowds of counter-protesters growing. When he asked Ruth how things were going in City Hall Park, she said fine. She said it was a long struggle, like abolition or universal suffrage.

"It's November," Mac said. "It could snow any day now. What happens when the weather really turns?"

She laughed, a raucous Ruth laugh that he hadn't heard in a while. "We're talking about Vermonters," she said. "Vermonters warmed by a little righteous indignation. And some good thermal sleeping bags. They'll be fine."

Thursday morning at the library, Silverman buzzed with excitement, "Did you hear about Berkeley last night? Dozens of protesters in skirmishes with police."

"Is that good?" Mac asked.

"It's all coming down, man. There are Occupy encampments now in fifty cities. They can't arrest everyone; they wouldn't have room in the jails. Something is going to have to give."

That afternoon, something gave.

At 2:00, Silverman jumped up from his laptop, where he had been tracking the news and his own texts, as usual. "I gotta go," he said. "Somebody's been shot in the park."

Mac heard about it that night from Ruth and Harper. They weren't there at the time; they were both still in school. But when they got to the park, they found that half of it had been cordoned off; there were cop cars everywhere.

"They said he shot himself," said Harper. "Right in the head. They said there was blood all over the inside of the tent." The man had died at the medical center that after-noon. Police were withholding his name, but they said he was 35 years old and "a transient."

"That's cop-talk," Ruth said. "God forbid they say 'homeless.' It sounds too 'political.'"

Mac asked, "Was he a protester?"

"Everyone in that park is a protester, one way or an-other. We don't know his story yet. But we'll find out more tomorrow."

Mac laid one hand flat on the dinner table. "You are *not* going back there tomorrow."

Ruth looked at him evenly. "You're not telling me what to do."

He paused. "You're right. You can do what you want with your own life. But you're not taking our daughter."

Harper looked back and forth. She knew she didn't have a vote.

The next morning, Mac saw Jocelyn Winters coming from a distance. He said to Silverman, "Here comes that woman you do not like." Silverman evaporated.

She did not say "I told you so." She did not address the situation in City Hall Park at all. She was fuming about more immediate matters.

"This is absurd," she said. "I don't know why I even bother." Her silver-blue eyes actually looked tired.

"What is it?" Mac asked.

"This morning in class, a student asked why I had posted an excerpt from *Alice in Wonderland* on reserve.

I said, 'What?' And she said, 'It's a scene where Alice meets Humpty Dumpty? It's really funny and all, but I'm not sure how it relates to public policy.'" Winters glared. "If this is your idea of a joke—"

Mac felt tired, too. He made a note without speaking.

Winters said, "Monkeying with online resources is an actionable offense. You—or your 'computer guy'—might want to review the Academic Integrity code." She laid on the air quotes heavily. Then she turned on her heel and left.

Silverman stepped out from behind a pillar. Scratching under both arms, he hooted like an orangutan. "It's actually *Through the Looking-Glass*," he said, "not *Alice in Wonderland*. Rookie mistake."

That afternoon, Mac picked Harper up from school, and, at her request, dropped her off at her friend Addie's house. Silverman was covering for him at work. City Hall Park was closed. It was another cold, rainy November afternoon.

Mac found himself driving up Williston Road. Just for the company.

Day 47. At least, he *thinks* it's Day 47. He may have lost a day in the storm. He is on his way again. The tooth has dulled into a steady ache, an empty space he cannot stop tonguing. With the return of calm weather, he tries to make up for lost time.

But he finds himself listless. He can't sustain his pace, and needs to rest more often than usual. Maybe it's just a natural lull. Shackleton reported going through such phases; he said he just had to push through them.

If it *is* Day 47, it is the winter solstice. He has brought Christmas gifts from Cecily and the Bean, small items in bright paper that he is to unwrap on that day, along with a brandied fruitcake. If his estimate is correct, he is only days away from the Pole. And yet he cannot whip himself to greater speed. Days pass, and the horizon stays the same.

When Christmas arrives (if it *is* Christmas), he opens his gifts—a pen from Cecily, a pearl-handled knife from The Bean—and sits by the fire. He gets drunk on fruitcake. He will push harder tomorrow.

Someday soon, he will arrive at the Pole. The still point in a turning world. It will be extraordinary. He will raise both fists above his head, and turn in a circle to survey the planet. He will see nothing but ice and pale blue sky. When he moves off into the future, whichever way he steps will take him North.

Mixty Motions

This is The Book of Emotions.

Acedia. Listlessness, lack of alacrity, spiritual hollowness.

Ambiguphobia. Fear of being misunderstood.

Ambivalence. The tendency to see everything with mixed emotions. Autumn in New England.

On the last day of his marriage, Mac McKenzie did chores. He cleaned both toilets in their little two-bedroom house—the one upstairs that he had shared with his wife and daughter for thirteen years and the half-bath downstairs, which Ruth had originally imagined as serving dinner guests. He went through all his junk in the basement, filling Hefty bags with dusty sports equipment and crates of old records and boxes of letters—God, remember when people wrote letters? Somehow he managed not to sit down and read any of them, or to dig out the old turntable and play "Astral Weeks" and "Hunky

Dory." He had to keep moving. There was so much to do.

He shook out the exhaust hose of the dryer, as he was supposed to do once a year and had not done since they moved in. It spumed out a spiral of lint. He carried his old weight-lifting bench to the front curb, where he set it next to Harper's plastic lawn mower, a hulking desktop computer, and boxes of ancient books. Against them he propped a hand-lettered sign reading "FREE."

The old double mattress, the one he and Ruth had used in the apartment on Murray Street, was too unwieldy for one person to haul up the stairs, even a big guy like Mac. He leaned it against a basement wall, and tried to brush the mildew off. After a brief, quiet lunch at the kitchen counter — it was a Sunday, so he tuned in the Red Sox pre-game on the radio — he went out and cut the grass, then did the weed-whacking all around the little back yard — a task he had promised to Ruth for months and then put off, put off, put off. In mid-afternoon she came out of her study and stood at the back door, where she gave him a quizzical look. He kept whacking. She shrugged and went back inside.

He straightened things in the shed — shears and shovels, spades and nearly-empty cans of paint — and took a long look at his hunting rifle, leaned in a corner, underneath a box of shells. He rescued only the big toolbox, which he carried out to his old green truck. Then he went back, and pulled a bottle of Bushmills from behind the dusty canoe; that went in the truck, too. At the property line, Bud Marriott leaned over the hedge and said, "A little late spring cleaning, Mac?" Mac smiled and nodded. "Ultra-late," he said.

Back at the shed, their old black lab, Sloppy Joe, snuffled around the seldom-used door. Mac said, "Let it be, boy. There's nothing in there for us."

At dinner, he spoke just enough to stay in the game. Harper was racketing on about this guy in her pre-Algebra class, what a great guitarist he was, how it wasn't fair that Mr. Mahan gave him so much grief just because he didn't always do the homework, he had more talent in his little finger than Don Mahan could even imagine. Her dark eyes flashed. She got so wound up about things these days. Her mother took the teacher's side. Eventually Mac said, "Well, honey, no matter what a genius you are, you still have to do the homework." She looked at him funny, but let it go.

Both parents put Harper to bed. Ruth said, "Lights out, big day tomorrow." In Ruth World, every day was big. She and Mac both knew that within minutes Harper would flick on the little book light her father had given her on her eleventh birthday, and then lie awake reading some trashy teen romance. They could outlaw electronic screens in the house, but they couldn't very well say no reading, could they?

At 2 a.m., when Mac got up from the daybed in his study and crept down the hall to his daughter's room, he found her keelhauled by sleep, a book lying open on her pillow, the little light throwing shadows on the wall. As always, the room bore the traces of Hurricane Harper.

Every surface was covered with piles of clothing, scattered school books, kicked-off shoes. This was one of the rare fights he had won: allowing her room to be its own nation-state. Everywhere else in the house, she had to pick up after herself; here she lived in a state of nature. There was a scent of something aromatic — patchouli? He didn't know, but it smelled legal. He looked at her for a long moment — bright blond hair rough-cut and long, the crooked nose that was broken at birth, long arms and legs askew like a stop-action windmill. Sloppy Joe was curled at her feet. She had arranged a footlocker so he could climb where he could no longer jump. Mac switched off the little light and stretched out beside her. She groaned and rolled over. Dog tags jingled. Then quiet.

He lay back and gazed at the ceiling, which was a deep blue littered with glow-in-the-dark stars. He and Harper had stuck them up there five years before. He had planned on classic constellations, but when Orion turned out more like Cap'n Crunch, they rolled their own. There was The Pepper Mill on the eastern horizon; above it he found The Wheelbarrow. Then there was The Escalator, and Downward Dog, and Addie (her best friend at the time), and, off on the western horizon, in splendid isolation, there was Harold, crayon brandished high. Straight overhead was a full moon with a lipsticked mouth and the dark skeptical eyes of her mother.

His chest was full of nails and salt. If it hurt this much, it had to be right.

Outside the open window, a soft rain started pattering

on the gingko leaves, like an old conversation resumed. Mac stood by the bed and whispered, "Come on, Joe, let's go learn us some new tricks." The dog clambered down from the bed.

Summer was ending again. In the dark kitchen, he could smell the peaches in the bowl by the fridge, the hot prickly fragrance of July living on into September. He put one in his jacket pocket. From a drawer he took a pair of scissors, and from his jeans he pulled a credit card. He cut it in half, and dumped the bits of plastic in the trash. He set the house keys on the counter, and then locked the door by pushing in the button on the knob before closing it. He would be hearing the click of that latch in his mind for a long time to come.

Out in the yard, the rain had already stopped. Sloppy Joe sniffed at the Japanese maple. Mac wanted to be like that: focused. Next meal, next squirrel, next butt. He thought he could make out the cool fragrance of calendula from Evie and Leah's garden across the street. God, Evie was going to lay into him for this. But he wouldn't be there to hear it.

He helped the dog into the cab of the truck — it took a little boost from below. Then he looked one more time under the tarp in back. Suitcase. Sleeping bag. Foam pad. Tool box. Bushmills. First-Aid kit. Sloppy's water dish. A fifty-pound bag of Dog Chow, Elderly Dog Formula. In the glove box there was a jar of Nutella. What else did you need? He pulled his phone from his jeans pocket, gazed at it briefly, and heaved it into the woods behind the house. Then he got behind the wheel and released the hand brake, so the old pickup would roll soundlessly down the driveway into Louise Street. By the time he started the engine, he was halfway down the block.

Anger.

Anxiety.

Appel du vide (French). The call of the void.

Awumbuk. The Baining people of Papua New Guinea use this term for the sadness felt when a visitor leaves. According to the Baining, awumbuk lasts for exactly three days, during which time you will be no good at either gardening or hunting. However, if you leave a coconut shell full of water sitting open in your house, it will soak up the awumbuk, which can then be disposed of safely.

Basorexia. The sudden desire to kiss someone.

Heading south out of Burlington, he stopped at a red light. They used to have flashing yellows overnight; when did that change? Through the open windows, crickets scraped on a light breeze. There was nobody on the road. No cops in sight. The light was still red. This was ridiculous. It was three freakin' o'clock in the morning. He gunned it, and the pickup roared for the highway.

Sloppy Joe yelped in the back of the cab, where Mac always kept an old horse blanket for his rides.

The highway was in full road construction mode, with orange barrels blocking off a lane where no discernible work was underway. Mac took aim. Fwap. Fwap. Fwap-

fwap-fwap-fwap: He took out a whole row of them. Then he put "Blonde on Blonde" in the CD player, and turned it up loud. All that brassy rage. He felt like Jack out with Milky White, striding the nut-strewn roads.

Not another day of fakery and waste, he told himself. Not another day.

This was for the best. Ruth and Harper would be happier without him moping around. Sloppy Joe was getting harder to handle; sad decisions were coming soon. This was for the best.

If the power went down, would Ruth know how to throw the circuit breaker? She'd figure it out.

As he drove down the dark highway into the mountains, Mac thought about entries for The Book of Emotions. His book. The one he had not been writing for ten years now, planned and imagined and always back-burnered. There should be a word, a positive word, for persistence in putting things off. Procrastenacity? For years he had accumulated notes for the book—little scraps of paper that he scribbled during meetings and on park benches, in coffee shops and waiting rooms. He had bought a beautiful notebook for the compilation, with a gilded cover and creamy unlined paper, The Notebook for The Book. So far, he had not sullied the snowfields of its pages. Instead, he stuffed under its cover these triple-folded slips of paper, discovered weeks or months later in the pockets of other seasons. *Collywobbles. Gladsomeness. Heebie-jeebies.* Some of the words remained undefined; some of the definitions went a bit askew. Maybe now, now that he would have time to himself, his own sweet time, he would get down to it.

Blues. Nobody loves me but my mother, and she could be jivin' too.

Crepuscularia. A predilection for dusklands.

Desire. Too big. Specify. Desire for another person, sexually? See *Lust*. For money? See *Greed*. For power? See *Megalomania*. Desire to publish a book, just one freakin' book, in your lifetime, so your name is preserved in the Library of Congress and somebody might find it, your book, in a Little Free Library one day, waiting patiently among the old romances and self-helpers for someone who might pick it up and think, "Hey, I didn't know Mac McKenzie wrote a book!"? See also *Yearning*.

When the sky started paling before them, they were ninety miles down the road, past Barre and Sharon and Quechee. At the garish interchange of White River Junction, he took the exit ramp. "Come on, Joe," he said. "Time to see a man about a horse."

They had got Sloppy Joe just a year after Harper was born, because Mac thought she should grow up with a dog. Ruth wasn't enthusiastic. As a professor of Environmental Studies, she was devoted to the natural world, but she was busy with her classes and conferences and activism. She and her comrades were just at the start of the fight against the parkway that was projected to slice down Pine Street, bringing streams of commuter traffic to their little neighborhood near town. Keeping up with a baby was hard enough; she didn't need a puppy to look after, too. Ruth was more flora than fauna, anyway. And dogs were so messy. But when Mac brought a bundle of scruffy black fur home from the shelter, she caved.

Of course, Ruth had her ideas about how a dog should be raised. No treats made of meat, because those things were created from God knows what kind of mistreated animals. No running free off the leash, even in the park, which was full of kids who would be terrified by this wild bounding thing twice as big as they were. And no climbing up on the furniture, especially the bed. She said that pets appreciated clear limits.

Mac wanted the puppy so badly that he conceded on all these points—and then, on the first night, Sloppy Joe whined so relentlessly from his crate downstairs that Mac rescued him before midnight. He took the puppy on his side of the bed, where it settled in and fell asleep within minutes, and only peed once. What was a little dog pee among friends? Mac changed the sheets in the morning.

Harper loved that puppy more than butterflies or Cheerios, and the feeling was mutual. In the first year, Ruth was always in a crouch, hands out like a linebacker, ready to protect her baby. But Mac knew that Sloppy knew: this little one was one of his people, not to be damaged. When other dogs approached her stroller in the park, he started growling before they even got close. He was Harper's TSA. And Harper, well, she knew, too. Sloppy was her slobbery sibling, a little too loud some-

times—when he barked, she backed off, looking doubt-
ful—but clearly on her team. Then she started barking
too. Ruth rolled her eyes at Mac.

"Ruff," he said.

One time, when Harper was ten, Sloppy went missing.
She was devastated. She took four of her T-shirts, rubbed
them against her torso, and laid them at the corners of
their little lot. Three weeks later he wandered home, and
never told anyone where he'd been.

That puppy was twelve years old now, with a geriatric
hobble and a salt-and-pepper muzzle. Mac helped him
out of the truck at a Waffle House. "It's OK, boy," he said,
running a hand over his own bristly chin. "I'm not shaving on this trip either." In the early years, Ruth loved it
when he had just shaved: she traced invisible lines on
his cheek with her fine-boned fingers and said, "You put
the *oo* in 'smooth.'" When they were courting, he sometimes shaved twice a day. "No more scraping," he said
to Sloppy Joe as the dog wet down the leg of a plastic
picnic bench at the edge of the parking lot. Mac cinched
the leash to a bicycle rack and promised to be back soon.

Inside, he squinted: the place was so bright with flu-
orescent-lit plastic and chrome that he thought of his
shades, still sitting on the dresser back on Louise Street.
He shrugged, and sat at the counter, just barely resisting
the urge to spin on the stool. Then he spun a little. The
dark hands of a clock on the back wall said 5:30. The smell
of ammonia from the overnight mopping said a.m. The
waitress looking up from a thick paperback said, "Hi."

At forty-three, Mac was way too old for her; he knew that. She was hardly older than Harper. She had the high cheekbones of some African tribe — probably the child of refugees. Her white plastic name tag said "Aasiya." She put a napkin in the pages of her novel. On the shiny cover was a design involving swords and chalices. Mac said, "What's that about?"

"Time travel," she said. She handed him a laminated menu.

"Ah," he said, nodding. He wanted everything on the menu. Belgian waffles, strawberries, whipped cream from an aerosol can, bacon and sausage and hash browns. And hash! And eggs, fried and poached and scrambled and coddled. And bacon, did he mention bacon? Gooseberries, if you got 'em. He ordered coffee.

When she brought it, in a heavy melmac mug, he asked, "What *is* time, anyway?"

She pointed at the clock and said, "Twenty to six."

He shook his head, looked at her novel, and said, "No, I mean, what is time?"

"Things change," she said. "Time is how we keep track."

He sat with his coffee. Ruth would be getting up soon, and finding that there was no coffee made in the kitchen. It was a sonofabitch thing to do, leave your wife and child. Mac had never been a sonofabitch; he didn't even use that kind of language most of the time. Most of the time, he was a reference librarian at the university, a little testy with his colleagues when they were being stupid, a little scary to undergraduates who didn't expect a rangy sandy-haired mountain man behind the counter, but sonofabitchery wasn't in his repertoire. So what was he doing?

Back in the truck, sitting in the parking lot, he gave Sloppy Joe a Slim Jim and ate his peach. He slurped; the dog gnawed. He was mighty tired. And he was so buzzed on burnt coffee and adrenaline, no way was he going to sleep anytime soon. His mouth was going to taste like bad coffee all day. Hell, maybe the rest of his life. The rest of his life? What did that mean? He didn't intend to brush his teeth. Where would he have brushed his teeth? Not in that god-awful Waffle House washroom. It smelled so bad in there that he had gone around the back of the building to pee against a wall.

One thing was damn sure. He wasn't turning around. He couldn't unstrike the drum. He punched Dylan back into the CD player and got off the highway, heading north on some two-lane state route. Highways were for losers.

Ennui.

Fear.

Guilt.

Hwyl (Welsh). Exuberance, gusto. Pronounced *who-eel*, it refers to a sailboat, the sensation of clipping along on the water, carefree. It is also a word for goodbye.

When Harper was in grade school, he was always the one who got home first, to be there when she got back from school, and then head off with her to the park down the street, with Sloppy Joe chasing squirrels all the way. Ruth was so busy in those years, always needing to stay at the office to see another student or catch up on e-mail or rally the troops against some environmental abuse, it was his time to give. But Harper was in junior high now, and she had places to be. Girlfriends to hang out with, maybe boyfriends, who knew? She had grown into the cloud of adolescence, with its sulky silences and its sudden outbursts, like her defense of that slacker guitar boy at dinner. She didn't need her old man anymore.

He and Ruth had nothing to say, and they kept saying it. He made up a little poem that he kept adding to in his mind.

He said Now
She said Never
He said Ocean
She said River
He said Both
She said Neither
He said Leeway
She said Laws
He said Why
She Because
He said Fiddle
She said Bow
He said May I
She said No

The sun was clear of the tree line now. The sky was poppied with clouds. The road went north.

Indignation.

Jocularia. The inclination to deflect serious things with a joke.

Kaukakaiuu (Finnish). Homesickness for a home where one has never lived.

Litost (Czech). According to Milan Kundera, *litost* is untranslatable. So the hell with it.

Love. How often do we really feel it? When I say "I love guacamole," how far is that from loving my mother or loving God or loving the whole bloody pulp of being alive? Does it have a shelf-life? How could I have believed so earnestly that I loved her? And yet I did. If you can fall into it, I guess you can also fall out.

He drove for a few hours. Scrub forest, little towns. The sun passed meridian. He was damn tired. He didn't know if this was Vermont or New Hampshire. Did it matter? On the outskirts of some little town, he pulled into the parking lot of a big concrete church. What day was it? Monday. They wouldn't mind if he took a little nap. He let Sloppy out to pee, then boosted the old guy up into the truck bed. Mac crawled in beside him, spread out the foam pad, punched the rolled-up sleeping bag into a pillow, and pulled the tarp over them both. This was the life.

Then something was pounding on his feet. Maybe it was the dog. Bedding down next to Sloppy was like sleeping with a sack full of hamsters.

"Hey, buddy."

The world rustled with a plastic crepitation. Then it burst with sunlight. Something or someone had pulled the tarp off.

"Hey, buddy."

Sloppy gave a tardy yip. What was pounding on his boots? He was too young to wake up. Who was hey-buddying him?

"You can't sleep here."

Well, that was true: he couldn't sleep *now*. He had been doing just fine before Hey Buddy came along.

"Can I see some I.D.?"

Oh, it was that kind of Buddy. Mac sat up and mumbled something about his wallet being here somewhere. He fumbled in his jacket, and found his driver's license.

Hey Buddy took it to his squad car. Mac looked at Sloppy Joe. "Some watchdog you are."

Sloppy Joe whined. "All right, so you can't smell in your sleep. I'll cut you a break this time. But you better start earning your keep, man. Don't forget: you're the dog."

Hey Buddy returned, and handed Mac the license. He was clearly disappointed. Mac made up a story about driving all night to visit friends in Newport, getting too tired to drive safely, and pulling over for some rest.

The cop nodded. "Well, you can't sleep here. This is private property."

Mac said, "All right, I'm feeling better now. I'll get back on the road."

Hey Buddy didn't budge. Mac bundled Sloppy into the cab, and got a police escort until he passed the town limits. Who-eel, Buddy.

Melancholy. Mood indigo.

Nostalgia. Longing for a golden age that never was. Or even if it was, what good is longing for it now?

Nullishness.

Oblivitude.

His whole life bore the watermark of failure. His father, the small farmer, wanted him to be a country lawyer, because that was what people with verbal skills did: they argued cases and wrote briefs and made satchels full of money. His mother wanted him to be a minister; he would deliver poetic sermons. The marriage to Ruth, a Jewish girl opposed to everything they stood for, had felt like fate. God, the marriage to Ruth.

He said Whiskey
She said Wine
He said Free verse
She said Rhyme
He said Why not
She said How
She said Never
He said Now

Sometimes when he got home from work and took Sloppy for a walk, he lingered at Evie and Leah's garden across the street, watching and chatting as Evie pulled weeds. She shook the short dark hair from her forehead and said he just needed to be patient. Harper would grow out of it; she was just like a baby that's teething. Ruth would loosen up after this project. Or the next one. Evie dropped a handful of weeds in a bucket.

Mac nodded. He thought, This is my life, my only life, burning in every moment.

Pique.
Pride.
Rage.
Shame.

Regret was his energy bar. He was hungry as a lumberjack. The truck was almost out of gas. Here was a gas station/diner. He pulled in.

"Most people just use Craig's List."

He was standing at a bulletin board next to the cash register of the diner while he waited for his hash browns. The girl who had taken his order was looking at him across the counter. Maybe he should sit down, but he was tired of sitting.

"Right. But I'm not Craig."

She smiled. Little crooked teeth. A small nose ring.

Long curly brown hair, unbrushed. Skinny, in jeans and a grey T-shirt, a yellowing apron. Maybe thirty. On her forearm a purple tattoo of a sword hanging from a thread. She looked tired. But who wasn't tired these days?

"So who are you then?"

"Jack," he said.

"I'm Lacey." She tugged the apron in a back-country curtsy. "Can you fry an egg, Jack?"

"Any way you want," he said. "Over easy, over hard, over medium, yolk broke, you name it."

"Sunny side up?"

"In a pinch."

"We could use somebody." She looked behind her to the kitchen. A tall guy with flared black sideburns was clattering around back there—hashing some browns, presumably. "When can you start?"

"Today," he said. "Just give me some eggs and a skillet."

"I'll talk to my husband," she said.

He took a paper cup full of water outside for Sloppy Joe, and ten minutes later she came out, too. When she saw the dog, she threw herself at him, engaging in an all-out all-fours tussle. Mac started to intervene, worried for Sloppy's fragile bones—but she knew what she was doing. She pinned him, and the dog whined with joy. Then she walked them both to a ramshackle bar down the road. Sloppy got the beef jerky. Lacey and Mac put the lime in the coconut.

Mac said, "Shall we have another?" The bar had a

garage-door type window that was rolled up to let the September sunlight in. It was sweater weather. Mac crossed his arms over his sweaterless chest.

She said, "Drinks are like tits."

His eyes widened.

"One's not enough, three are too many."

They had another. She told him her life story. Small town, big hopes, married young, never left.

Mac listened. That's what he did. For fifteen years, Ruth had been the talker, and that was OK with him. Was this a sign of empathy, or was it just laziness? Maybe both. Maybe he wasn't binary.

Torschlusspanik. (German) Literally, "door-shutting-panic." Anxiety about being too late, too late, too late.

He got up to check the jukebox, over by the door. She got up, too, and they did a little silent two-step on the creaking floorboards. His blood was roaring; he felt as spastic as Joe Cocker. She took his elbow to turn him into her, and kissed him under the jaw, more nuzzle than kiss, more promise than nuzzle. The heat of it blossomed through his limbs.

He said, "Your eyes are bluer than robins' eggs."

"Your poetry is lousy," she said.

He said, "Well, I'll be damned."

She smiled.

"Your husband?" he said.

"Oh, we've been split for years. I just mention him for

protection, until I see what I'm dealing with. If you hadn't asked, you'd be drinking alone tonight."

He was a strike-anywhere match. He knew it couldn't end well. But what does?

Unease.
Vanity.
Wist.

At her apartment building, they left Sloppy Joe out in the sunshine, unleashed in the fenced-in yard. Inside, she pulled out all the stops. Well, she pulled out two of the stops. She lit tea candles all around the bed, and she put Van Morrison on the iPod. His mama told him there would be days like this.

She was flat-chested and sleek and skinny as a whippet. He didn't want to think of the dog image, but what can you do? Try not to think of a zebra, and suddenly your mind fills up with stripes.

It had been so long. He wanted to hold back, he wanted to make it last, he wanted—

Well.

He started to apologize. She put a finger to his lips. Sexiest thing that happened all afternoon. Then she scratched behind his ears.

So of course he fell asleep. Some time later, he heard a door opening, and then a voice in the next room. A female voice. Not Lacey's. She was still there beside him.

"Oh jeez," she said. "He's home."

He?

She threw on a robe and said, "Just clean up, and come out when you're ready."

He would never be ready. When he did step out into the living room, he found Lacey saying goodbye to an older woman, who was introduced as Lacey's mother. She hardly gave Mac a second look. She was intent on a dark-haired boy who was playing with a racecar on the floor.

"'Bye, Finn! See you tomorrow!"

The boy remained focused on his car, and she left. Finn looked about five years old, pale and thin. And he had some kind of problem. There was something strange about his eyes. Autism? Mac didn't know. He squatted by the boy and said, "That's a cool car. How fast can it go?"

The boy scurried over to the window, as far from Mac as possible. Mac said, "Hey, buddy," and started over to join him, but Lacey stopped him with a hand on his forearm.

"It's OK, Jack. You don't have to charm him."

He winced. "But—"

She was looking at the boy, who had huddled with his car beneath the window. And Mac saw, in that gaze, that she would never love him, Mac or Jack or Sazerac, with anything like the love she poured on Finn.

She turned back to him. "You charmed *me*," she said. "That was enough."

X. The unknown.

Yearning. "Longing, we say, because desire is full of endless distances."

Zeal. Always a new land, on the horizon.

She made him a sandwich for the road. She didn't say Call me. He didn't say I'll call you. When he got back outside, Sloppy was thrilled to see him. The air was cool: September leaning into October. He shrugged on his jacket.

Who was he kidding? He was never going to write a book. Those notes would accumulate forever. Until they didn't. He hoisted the dog into the truck. It would be evening soon.

On Louise Street, the day was ending, too. Clouds' bellies were touched with pink. Harper wasn't home yet. Her mother stood at the kitchen window, watching the color fade. She turned back into the kitchen. There were papers to grade for tomorrow.

Addlement, misery, and wonder. Yolk broke, over and over. He managed not to turn back for Burlington. But only just.

In the Meantime

How much sleep does a person need? If you're a young parent or a medical intern, the answer is probably as much as you can get. If you're recovering from an illness or hunching into your final years, let it be as much as you want. They say that sleep cleanses the brain, flushing out the detritus of the day. But if you're a healthy teenager, do you really need to sleep into the afternoon?

Leah and I were talking about this after dinner, in our back room—the room we added because we were drowning in clutter. Would it have been easier, and cheaper, to de-clutter the rest of the house? Yes. Did the new room, with its many windows, its pale hardwood floor, its pot-bellied stove and reading nook, quickly become cluttered, too? Of course. But we didn't have any illusions, when we had that room built, about changing our essential characters. Some people were born for clutter. Now we had more room for it.

When I say "we," of course I mean "I." Left to her own devices, Leah would keep a house neat and sleek. The other day, when I left yet another unfinished project — is there any other kind? — on the only open desk space of the study, she said, "Evie Morrison, you're a magilla."

I said, "Yes, but I'm *your* magilla."

"I'm going to call FEMA."

"Say hi for me."

We both know she'd hate it if things got too neat around here. She'd miss the complaining.

We were having tea after dinner — well, I was having hot water, as usual — and talking about sleep. The topic was inspired by Harper, the fifteen-year-old daughter of our across-the-street neighbor, Ruth. Lately, Harper seemed to do nothing but sleep. Twelve hours a day, fifteen hours a day: if she didn't have to go to school, she might never leave her bed. Ruth said that on weekends the blinds in Harper's bedroom never got opened.

"It's not natural," I said to Leah, picking up my cup of hot water. "It's like she's been cursed, like Snow White or Sleeping Beauty."

Leah said, "Actually, it's completely natural. And those stories are perfect comparisons."

Leah teaches literature at the community college. I knew I was in for some elucidation. "How?" I asked.

"Snow White and Sleeping Beauty are classic teenage girls. Teenage girls need a lot of sleep. Everything they do is exhausting. Their bodies are changing, which takes a lot of energy all by itself. They can't do anything about it — but they agonize over it as if they *could* do something. That's exhausting, too. And everyone around them is also freaking out about those changes—boys, parents, all the girls they know, who are going through the same thing. I get tired just thinking about it. So what's the most logical and useful response? A nice long nap. Don't you remember being a teenager?"

"Well, it wasn't exactly yesterday. But I don't think I was sleeping a lot. Remember, I was captain of the volleyball team, and president of Student Council, on my father's fast track to college. And I was also trying to fend off Jason Horowitz, and wondering why I had those feelings about Janie Moffett. Who had time to sleep?"

"Well, you might have been better off if you'd done a little Sleeping Beauty routine."

"But Sleeping Beauty is just lying there, waiting for a Prince! How is that a good role model? And that guy who's been hanging around Harper? That Josh dude? I assure you, he's no prince." I had seen this guy with her down in the park at the end of our block—dressed all in black, snarly dark hair over his eyes, a cigarette in his hand. "He looks like an executioner's apprentice. Elly Taylor says he grew up in the Jackson Terrace apartments without a mother, and he got picked up once for breaking and entering, but released as a juvenile."

"Wait: Elly Taylor is our authority now?" Elly was a widow down the street, and she had been known to embroider on her stories. "And are we being a little classist in that assumption about Jackson Terrace?"

"OK, OK, I'm a bad person."

"The thing is," she said, "the Prince is no prince either."

"What do you mean?"

"I mean, the Prince in those stories is just a square jaw and a cape. He has no name, no personality. He arrives at the glass coffin or the tower bedroom, and he manages to wake the sleeping girl, but otherwise, he's a big zero. Can you remember anything else about him?"

"Um, he's a good dancer?"

"Right. And we know what the dance signifies."

A youth full of Disney worship went clank in my brain. Leah continued.

"But the heart of the story isn't the handsome dimwit or the cute little dwarves; it's the sleep itself. The adolescent girl *needs* that withdrawal, that period of gestation."

"So Harper is just doing what's best for her."

"Maybe so."

Leah got up and carried the tea tray to the sink, where she started doing the dinner dishes. We continued the conversation across the breakfast bar. I wasn't ready to let it go.

"But it's driving her mother crazy! You know Ruth: she's busy with a thousand things. She doesn't know what to do with a zombie down the hall."

"I know." Ruth taught Environmental Studies at the university, and had a hand in all kinds of community activism. She used to haul Harper to every march or rally; now she couldn't get her out of bed.

"So what can we do about it?"

"Maybe we should sleep on it." Leah hung the dish

towel over the handle of the oven door. "I've got to do some reading. You're walking Kinsey, right?"

"Right." I sat back with my cup of hot water, which was quite cool now.

Leah and I once thought seriously about having a child of our own. We had friends who were successful with artificial insemination. I think I would have been the one to bear the child. I was the homebody; Leah was always leaning into her next literature class or writing project, and sometimes she got involved with Ruth in community work, like the fight against the big new development downtown. But every time we started to discuss it, life got crazy again—for Leah with her teaching, for me with my job as a guidance counselor at a private high school— and we shelved the topic again. We got Kinsey, a sweet little terrier mix who kept us running every day. We were happily connected to my nephews and Leah's nieces. We barely had time for our lovely circle of friends.

Besides, we had Harper, right there on Louise Street. We had known her forever, starting with that epic home birth, when we stood in the wings with Mac, the anxious father, eager to help but unable to do a thing. Did Ruth's screams of agony have anything to do with our loss of interest in childbearing? We didn't talk about it.

And then we watched Harper grow up, from close range. We knew her first as a little blond dervish, splashing in the wading pool, getting into everything. I said to Leah, "Maybe a little hyperactive?" She said, "You think?" Then she was The Little Mermaid, mesmerized by Ariel's yearning for a whole new world. She wasn't allowed any screen time at home, but when we babysat, she never failed to sucker me into bringing over the DVD. I told her this had to be our little secret from her mother. That made it even sweeter.

At the same time, she was Daddy's Little Monster. That was one of Mac's names for her, and she was happy to oblige. Sometimes it was cute. He got her a hat with Sendak horns, and they played Wild Things in their little back yard. Sometimes, though, when she was crying inconsolably about a lost toy or an unfair restriction, the nickname felt a little close to the bone. Mostly, he called her Bean, or Sprout, because that's how she grew. In group photos from school, she towered over her classmates, a burst of blond dishevelment in the back row.

Gradually, she grew apart from us. There was a frou-frou phase in fifth or sixth grade, when she was inseparable from her BFF Addie, a pert little girl from a big house two blocks up the hill. Once I saw the two girls at Barnes & Noble, camped out in the Romance section. Mac was probably downstairs in Sports. Actually, I smelled them before I saw them: I noticed this awful fruity perfume from about twenty feet away, and looked over to see the tall blonde and the shorter brunette, standing with paperbacks open against the shelf, so immersed in their books and their cloud of cat civet that they never looked up to see me. I had never known Ruth to wear a whisper of scent. For about fifteen minutes that year, Harper changed her name to Zora.

Then Addie grew boobs, and the boys started flocking, and Too Tall Harper was left in her dust. One day I saw her sitting on the swing set in the park, where she and Addie used to sit side by side. Her father was on a nearby bench, reading something. I went over and took the empty swing.

"Mind if I sit?" I asked.

"No." Her voice was utterly flat.

What are you thinking about?"

"Nothing."

"Where's Addie?"

"How would I know?"

Man, you couldn't pay me enough to live through junior high again.

Even then, sleep was a problem—but in a different way. For years, Harper just refused to go to bed. Or refused to stay there. Ruth often told me about it the next day when she got home from work, as I puttered in our front garden. Every night, an hour or two after bedtime, Harper appeared at her parents' door, asking to be taken into their bed. Sometimes they let her climb in; sometimes one of them (usually Mac) went to lie down with her for a while. She only wanted company. Ruth thought maybe it was their fault, for having no other children.

Maybe Harper's Sleeping Beauty shtick wasn't so strange after all. Maybe she was making up for lost time.

In our house, I'm the bad sleeper. Most nights, Leah

turns off her reading light before eleven, gives a good-night pat to Kinsey, who sprawls between us on the bed, and rolls away from us. Soon I hear her breath coming more slowly. Meanwhile, I sit up with a mystery or a police procedural under my own book light. Sometimes I manage to turn out the light by one o'clock; sometimes I get up to watch a recorded episode of "The Voice" in the guest room downstairs. I have arranged a special dispensation at work: no appointments before ten a.m. Who wants to talk to a guidance counselor before that, anyway? Leah takes Kinsey for her morning walk and then gets away to her early class. Often she leaves me a little note about the day to come—a day she is already living in, and which I can't face yet.

I don't know how much Harper's trouble had to do with Ruth's cancer—but it can't have helped. They found the first tumor when Harper was ten. Ruth went through radiation and chemo, and had a breast removed. Then the cancer emerged in the other breast. Since it was small, she opted against a second surgery. She said she could manage it with what they call "watchful waiting"—frequent scans and consultations, monitoring it month by month. She said she was too busy to go under the knife again.

You might think that such an experience would bring mother and daughter closer—but only if the mother lets it happen. Ruth was so stoic, she wanted to manage it all by herself. She wanted to stay at work, not be a burden to anyone. She couldn't seem to grasp that people *want* to share your burden. At least, people who love you do. Your daughter and your husband, your across-the-street neighbors, want to know how you're doing, and want to help. Maybe it's true, in some absolute sense, that you're ultimately on your own. But we don't live in the ultimate. We live in the meantime. The generous thing is to let people help.

Of course, this is easy for me to say. When you hurt, it's hard to be generous.

Increasingly, the household battles were between mother and daughter. Mac agreed on all the principles — limiting Harper's screen time, making sure she ate a healthy diet, restricting her outings for safety's sake — but no one could doubt that Ruth was the source of those principles, and also the prime enforcer.

I said to Leah, "If Mac could stop being The Cool Parent for a minute, he might see that Harper really needs more discipline."

She said, "That's like asking Mitch McConnell to stop being a weasel. Reasonable — but how likely?"

And then Mac left. Just like that, now you see me now you don't. Ruth's cancer was stable at the time. Harper was thirteen. Neither of them wanted to talk about it. Ruth put her head down and focused on her teaching and her community work. And Harper? She also seemed to go back to her routine — school, skateboarding, being a kid. Maybe they both thought Mac would come back sooner or later. He kept not coming back.

Eventually, inevitably, Josh came along. I wish I knew

more about him. Although Harper and I had stayed on friendly terms, stopping to chat on the street, she clearly didn't want to talk about Josh. When I was her age, I wasn't eager to confide in adults about such things, either. I saw them in the park, or at the bus stop down on Pine Street. I heard things from Elly Taylor, who stopped by my garden to gossip. I think he was the first real boyfriend. So why was she sleeping all the time?

One of the reasons Ruth was always happy about me and Leah as babysitters was that like her, we're sticklers about language. Up at the university, Ruth has a sign on her office door that proclaims, "You Are Now Entering a 'Like'-Free Zone." Leah has her English teacher chops, and I've been coaching kids on their college application essays for over twenty years. I have even developed a little reputation as Grammar Girl. "You are *not* going to lay down," I tell students, "unless you are laying *something* down." They look at me as if to say, "Really? You're going to be like that?" And I look at them as if to say, "Do you want to get into college or not?"

Harper was a tough case. About a month after her father left, we sat at the table in our back room and talked about it. Or tried to talk about it. She had been largely silent since that October morning when she woke up to find that he was gone, leaving a flimsy note about how this was best for everyone. He was also taking Sloppy Joe, their beloved old black Lab. He seemed to think this was a mercy, because Sloppy was on his last legs.

I asked Harper if her father's departure had been a complete surprise.

She looked out at the wan November afternoon and twisted a long lock of hair in one hand. "Like, totally," she said. "I was literally shocked, like, out of my socks."

I couldn't help myself. "Really?" I said. "You felt an electrical current that made your socks pop off?"

She scowled. "You know what I mean."

"I think I do," I said, "But I wish you would *say* it. Literally."

"OK," she said. "Yes, I was surprised."

"What about in retrospect? Does it still seem surprising that he would leave?"

"Well, no. They weren't much of a couple, were they?"

I let that stand as a rhetorical question.

"I guess I've known for years," she said. "Once, I like, asked Dad —"

I tisked, and she frowned. "English," I said.

"This *is* English!" she said. "It's just not *your* English." But she started again. "I asked Dad why they got married. It was one of Addie's Big Life Questions. And he went all deep on me. He said that when they got married, he felt like" — she paused, as if waiting to be corrected.

"'Like' is perfectly acceptable in a comparison," I said.

"It's too complicated!"

"Life is complicated," I said. "He felt like what?"

She paused. Outside our windows, the afternoon was sinking towards dusk. "He felt like Mom was his Fate. That gave me the heebie-jeebies."

"Why?"

"Because! You don't get married just because you've got this cosmo-rama idea about it! That's like a romance novel. A bad one."

I smiled, and she went on.

"I don't believe in fate."

"Why not?"

"Because . . ." I could see her scanning for "like"s and "literally"s ahead of her, like a minesweeper clearing a path. "Because it's just an excuse to do something you're going to do anyway. Go ahead and do it, go ahead and marry the wrong woman if you want—but don't blame it on some outside force." She held both hands above her head, like a mime pushing against an invisible bubble. "Just do your thing," she said, "and own it."

That sounded more like Ruth than anyone I knew.

Then came the season of lies.

At least, according to Ruth they were lies. Harper said she had watered the garden, and Ruth found the flower beds and the watering can dry. Harper said she had done her homework, and Ruth saw on the school's website that no homework had been recorded in weeks. When confronted, Harper angled off into equivocations. She said the garden must have dried quickly, the homework was stupid, school a waste of time.

Back when she was in grade school, three blocks from home, Mac walked her there almost every day. Now she was at the combined junior and senior high, clear across town. And there was no Mac. In a budget crunch—as always—the school district decided to streamline its bus service by having kids from our near-town neighborhood take the city bus, swiping an ID card as they got on board. The bus stop, down by Jackson Terrace, wasn't far—but now, in her Sleeping Beauty phase, Harper started missing the bus regularly. She didn't want to get up. She didn't want to go to school. She said the bus was gross. She told stories of strap-hangers—those morning buses are crowded—rubbing up against her. Some days, Ruth drove her, though it wasn't convenient for her own work schedule; some days Ruth got robo-calls from the principal's office, reporting Harper's absence. Harper said she was present. Everybody knew, she said, those calls were unreliable. Ruth was busy with her teaching and environmental work, not to mention the quiet vigil over her own body. And whatever she felt about Mac. She was at the end of her rope. That's when I stepped in.

It was January; a new semester had just begun. One night at dinner, in the warm track lights of our back room, I said to Leah, "We've got to help Ruth."

"But Ruth doesn't want help."

"I know. But I've figured out a way. We take in Harper."

Leah considered. "How will that help? We can't force her to report for home room."

"Actually, we could—but this will be better. You know she's not happy at home. A change of venue will work wonders. She'll sleep regular hours, and we can make sure she gets to the bus on time. There are two of us." I've always been a problem-solver.

Leah didn't say what we were both thinking—that I wouldn't be the one making sure Harper got on the 7:30 bus. She can be so generous.

"One condition," she said. "Not the guest room."

"What?" We have a nice little guest room, right next to the downstairs bathroom. It would be perfect for an extended stay. "Where else would she sleep?"

Leah looked over at the reading nook. It's not a separate bedroom, or even a full-size bed, but I can attest, from many an afternoon nap, that the long cushioned bench is exceedingly comfortable. Still, I asked, "Why?"

"She needs to know it's temporary. She needs to know she's in the middle of our lives, and she can't just close the door and hide. You want her to make the 7:30 bus? I'll be banging around the kitchen every day at 6:45."

The logic was impeccable. Ruth said yes; she was desperate for change. Harper acquiesced; whatever got her mother off her case.

I laid out some sheets and blankets and pillows. We went over the house rules, which were pretty simple. Harper had to keep this corner of our back room neat. She would do her own laundry, down in our basement. She would walk Kinsey once a day, which pleased her; she missed old Sloppy Joe so much. If she wanted to listen to music, she would use earbuds. She had to be in bed by eleven. And she had to be up by seven. It would have been difficult to sleep in, anyway. The back room has no blinds, and even at that benighted season, daylight was rising by then. The room is separated from our kitchen only by the breakfast bar, so when Leah and Kinsey went clattering in, there was no escaping the noise. She would spend some time with her mother on the weekend. She winced at that, but nodded.

We gave her a house key, so she could let herself in after school if neither of us was home yet. We were all hopeful.

Within a few days, there was an odd morning note from Leah.

"Harper off to school, no problem. Didn't have time to clean the floor. Sugar?"

I had already experienced what she meant, as I walked across the kitchen in my slippers: something granular underfoot, scattered on the floor. We keep it as clean as we can; we don't want to encourage insects or mice. I got down on my hands and knees; my flannel pajamas and woolen robe gave me a little cushion. I wasn't crazy about testing the sugar hypothesis, but I figured the taste of a moistened fingertip wouldn't kill me. Sugar it was.

In the cupboard, the Domino's box was also surrounded by fallen grains. I sponged that up and swabbed the floor.

Then I turned on the electric kettle, and checked my phone. I was dimly aware that a call had arrived while I was still in bed; I had let it go to voice mail and rolled over. Now, with the taste of sugar still on my tongue, I played the message.

It was an automated call from the high school. "Your family member" — here a human voice filled the gap with a name—"was not present in home room this morning. Please let us know if we can be of further help." When I had described this process to Leah, she said, "Isn't that Ruth's job?" But I had told Ruth that if we were responsible for getting Harper off to school, we should receive those calls.

I called the principal's office. I told the administrative assistant this couldn't be right, because I knew Harper was on the bus to school at 7:30. The assistant sounded tired; she had clearly heard this before. She said, "She wasn't in home room. We think families should know." I realized that I was dealing with a bureaucracy—a big school, a person who had never met Harper—and felt bad for everyone involved. I looked forward to clearing it up with Harper.

At the dinner table that evening, she said, "My home room teacher doesn't like me."

Leah asked, "So she just marks you absent?"

"I guess so."

I said, "But you were there."

"Yes! Don't you believe me?"

The thing is, I didn't. Why would any teacher arbitrarily get a student in trouble that way? But what could I say to Harper's plaintive question? I said of course I believed her, but I had trouble imagining that the teacher could be so mean.

"She doesn't like me."

"Why not?"

"I don't know. Maybe she can tell that I think she's lame."

Leah said, "That might do it."

I said, "You might try to hide that. Teachers are sensitive too, you know."

Harper shrugged. I didn't entirely blame her. Here I was encouraging her to be dishonest, to cover up her true feelings. Maybe she just had a higher standard for herself.

I forgot to ask about the sugar. But the next morning, my slippers went crunch again on the kitchen floor, and the note from Leah read, "Put H on the bus. What's with the sugar?"

I cleaned it up, but I didn't have much time to ponder it, because I knew there was another new voice mail on my phone. It was another of those calls.

I called again, and had the same conversation with the same tired assistant. I couldn't help imagining that it would lead to the same conversation with Harper that evening. I asked if the home room teacher had an office hour that day.

That afternoon, it was easy to block out some time on my calendar—January is not a crunch time for guidance counselors—and drive to the high school to see Ms. Abbott. She was keeping a solitary office hour in her classroom, sitting at the big wooden desk. I squeezed into a tablet-chair beside it.

"Harper McKenzie?" she said, and looked at her book. "She's been absent eight days out of ten so far."

Ms. Abbot was young—maybe thirty—with a dark bob and a tan sweater set. The sort of young professional who inspires either confidence or envy. I decided to opt for confidence, and went right to the nub.

"She says she has been present. She says you don't like her."

Ms. Abbott smiled. "I'm sorry, Ms. Morrison, but I barely know her. I have thirty-five students in home room. Many of them, including Harper, don't take a class with me, so the ten minutes of calling the roll and making announcements is my whole time with them. We just started the new semester two weeks ago. I try to get to know them all—but it takes time. And when they're absent . . ." She waved a meaningful hand.

"I understand," I said. Whatever else this young woman might be, she was not lame. "Thank you for your time."

I drove home, earlier than usual. It was a dark and drizzly afternoon, on the verge of snow. I let Kinsey out in our fenced-in back yard; I didn't feel like walking her in the wet cold. Instead, I sat in the reading nook. It had been neatly made up that morning, sheets and blankets drawn tight.

Where was Harper going? Why was she lying? Should we discuss it with Ruth? Leah would have said of course we should; this was a mother's business. But I didn't see how it would help. It would just infuriate Ruth, make Harper more defensive, and undermine her confidence in us. In me.

I was stirred from my reverie by an unusual noise. A faint thumping, dim but steady, it seemed to come from right below me. Under our fair pine floorboards. How could that be? The back room doesn't have a full basement.

But it does have a crawl space, accessible from the deeper part of the basement through a little door high in the wall. The noise continued. Had Leah set an animal trap down there? Or maybe it was an untrapped creature, making its nest. Maybe it was two of them humping, creating more. Our neighborhood is famous for skunks and groundhogs, invaders of our gardens. I didn't want to find out.

But I had to look.

The single dangling lightbulb was already on, which was odd: we were usually careful about saving electricity. I knew that its dim glow wouldn't reach into the darker corners, so I snagged the flashlight from its hook by the stairs. It was cold down there, and smelled of detergent and mold.

I made my way past the washer and dryer, and turned toward the little door to the crawl space. In the shadows cast by the flashlight, I saw that a couple of boxes had been set up beneath it. Or maybe they had been there all along. The thumping grew louder.

I got up on the boxes and pulled the door open. It should have been pitch-dark inside. But almost immediately I saw a little rectangle of light.

I wouldn't have believed there was room for a person to fit in there, but she was sitting hunched over her phone, with her knees folded up to one side, a posture that only an adolescent or a yoga master could hold for long. She was facing away from the door, so for a second her foot kept thumping to some beat in her earbuds. Then she seemed to sense something, and looked up. The furnace churned behind me. In the sudden beam of the flashlight, her face was a blank. Next to her on the bare plank floor was a cereal bowl from our cupboard. I was sure I would find that it was full—or not so full, now—of sugar.

Part of me felt relieved that it wasn't something worse. Part of me felt guilty: why did I have to butt in?

She climbed down, and followed me upstairs. She was wearing the big down coat in which she had left the house that morning, now dusty with crawl-space grit. We sat at the dining table.

In the early dark of that wet afternoon, I saw our reflections in the black glass behind Harper. She slouched in the chair, so I saw my own face above the back of her blond head.

Her face was flat. Go ahead, it seemed to say. Go ahead and lecture me. You can't hurt me any more than I've already been hurt.

I asked about the sugar. She seemed a bit surprised by this opening, but said that in the night she had helped herself. Sitting on the floor? She nodded.

I said, "Leah put you on the bus," and she nodded again. "But you got off somewhere and wandered until I would be off to work. Then you came back here."

She made a barely perceptible nod, more with the eyes than the chin.

"But you were afraid that one of us would come home and find you too early in the day."

Again, the nodding look.

I said, "But it's skeevy in the basement!"

She shrugged, as if she hadn't noticed.

"When the time came," I said, "you could crawl out the half-door into the side yard and pretend you were just getting home."

She looked out the window. This ventriloquized confession was giving her less room to lie.

"No more eating sugar on the floor," I said. "If you want sugar, eat it here at the table, like a human being."

She nodded.

"And you've got to go to school."

She looked into her lap.

"What's wrong with school?" I knew it was a dumb question, but I still thought it had to be asked.

She looked up with the same flat eyes, as if to say What's *not* wrong with school?

I let the silence sit.

Then she said, "Josh."

In that one syllable lived a whole history of hope and grief and loss. I could only imagine what kind of meanness that boy had inflicted on her. But maybe there was meanness on her side, too. There was a lot of it going around.

It was clear that she didn't want to say anything more, not yet. She looked at her lap. I looked at our reflections. I decided to cut her a deal.

"If you go to school," I said, "every damn day"—I paused for effect—"I won't tell anyone about this. Not your mother. Not Leah. Not even Elly Taylor."

She couldn't help herself: she smiled. A little light came into her eyes. Her nod was faint, but it seemed real.

That night in our bedroom, I told Leah about the kitchen floor. Imagine sitting on the cold tile, when there are perfectly good chairs at hand. But I didn't tell her, or anyone else, about the crawl space. That was Harper's, and mine. It wasn't much. But it felt like one of the best things I've ever done. Like, literally.

Lying in our bed that night, I thought about the girl in our reading nook, just a floor below. I hoped she was sleeping an enchanted sleep. But maybe she was lying awake now, too.

THE GIANT'S WIFE

When I lie awake at night, listening to the furnace kick in and out, I make lists in my head.

Fold Mrs. Hosper's sheets
Refill detergent machine
Order more punch cards
Greek yogurt
Plant vitamins
Dentist
Xmas cards for Dee and Rastus

And when I get out of bed, I always say "Hello, big guy." First thing. I stopped saying it for a while ten years ago, after Carl died. But then one day I woke up and decided to say it anyway. I had shaped my life around that man, and now there's a Carl-sized hollow. Dead or alive, he's still with me.

And then I go to work. Every day. I open the All-Kleen at 6:30, because you need to be available to people before their own work day begins. It's just a short drive into town, and I've got the four-wheel drive for these icy days in December. Everybody in northeastern Vermont drives a Subaru, or else a truck. I'm on duty until Dee's granddaughter Roweena comes in for the evening shift at 3. If it's busy, I'll stay until 5 or so. Roweena is a sweetheart, but she can be spacy. I don't mind. Work is what I'm for.

It's silly to send Christmas cards to Dee and Rastus, because I see them all the time, and I'm not a Christmas person. All that fluster and obligation just depresses me. But they send cards to me, and what the hell, they're my friends, I can write a couple of cards.

So I'm sitting in my office on a Sunday morning, early, writing my two Christmas cards and not calling the dentist, when this guy walks in. He's big and unchiseled, but he moves like he used to be an athlete: he's got that lope. He's maybe forty-five, with a ten-day beard and sparse sandy-red hair. And a harried look, like something is chasing him. I mean, this guy is a frayed shoelace. You can't help noticing that kind of person; you wonder what's up with him. He heaves a bedsheet full of laundry up on the sorting table.

Carl never liked it that I opened early on Sunday, or at all—he said it was the Lord's day. So according to you, I said, the Lord intended Sunday for hunting and watching football? He said I was being stroppy—a Carl word, and it wasn't a compliment. But I knew he wasn't going to stop me, because the All-Kleen was our golden goose. At first it was just something to keep me busy after Jessie left, but soon it was bringing in enough to pay for a second car, so Carl didn't have to drop me off every morning on his way to the mill. This was back when the mill was still open, not just a shell of bricks casting shadows on the river. I told him, some people like to get things done on Sunday morning, some people are just busy all the other days, and you've got to cater to them. Did he really think the Lord was against getting your clothes clean on Sunday? Carl didn't care for loose talk about what the Lord likes and doesn't like, as if the Lord was just one of your neighbors who doesn't go for spicy foods. But he let me do my thing. In those first years after Jessie left, he didn't say much. All the king's horses and all the king's men.

Anyway, this guy comes in on a Sunday, early, when there's no one else in the place. I really like this quiet time, because I can catch up on chores, and sometimes I just watch an old video on the VCR in my office, where I can see the whole laundromat over the half-door that looks out toward the street. When the bell chimes over the front door, I look up and see this big guy, almost as big as Carl was, and I hit the pause button on "Terminator." I love all the Terminator movies, but the first one is definitely the best. Carl would say "How can you watch that again? Don't you know it by heart?" But some things just get better with repetition. You notice the little details, like those four beats of the bass drum every time the Terminator comes onscreen. I'm a little peeved about pausing it so close to the big fight scene—but, well, I'll be back.

I step out to greet the guy, who has emptied his bed-sheet on the table and started sorting through a pretty motley collection of duds. His ears are even redder than his hair, because it's five below zero outside. Already. Two and a half weeks before Christmas. He's wearing an old tan corduroy coat that's way too light for the weather, and I say "How can you stand it without a hat?" You know, in a motherly way. People usually appreciate that you care enough to say something. But this guy just shrugs, like he's embarrassed about being underdressed but he doesn't want to talk about it, doesn't even want to complain about the ridiculous cold. Most people can talk about the cold in this place all morning and into the afternoon. This guy, he just shrugs and goes back to sorting his stuff. Maybe he's feeling bad about having to do his laundry in a tired little laundromat on a Sunday morning. Maybe he doesn't want me to see the stains on his sheets. Maybe he just doesn't like small talk, I don't know. Once you've said hello and made yourself avail-able, sometimes you just have to get out of the way.

But then I notice, just outside the plate-glass window that fronts on Park Street, that his truck is still running, churning out exhaust in the frigid morning air. And I just have to say something, because that makes me crazy. We're in hock to the Arabs for their oil, and we've already fouled the air and water to the max, and still people want to run their engines all the time, it's insane. Maybe he thinks it's just going to take two minutes to get his laun-dry going and then he'll duck back out to the warm cab for whatever else he's going to pack into his Sunday morning. But I know it's going to take him at least ten minutes to sort his stuff and figure out the system and buy his tokens and detergent—I can see that he didn't bring his own—and well, I just can't stand it. But just when I'm about to say something a little bitchy about our nice clean air here in Lunenburg, I look one more time at the truck and I see movement in the passenger seat. A big black dog.

And that makes me even crazier. You can do your lousy laundry on Sunday morning, and you can shrug off the old lady who wants you to wear a hat, but you cannot leave your dog in the truck when it's five below zero. Even with the heater on. Even if you think it's just going to be two minutes. Not in my parking lot.

I try it the nice way. "Sir?" I say. It's weird calling somebody barely half your age "Sir," but so it goes; I'm in the sir-vice industry. He looks up from his whites, which aren't so terribly white if you want to know the truth, and I nod at the truck. "You can bring your dog in. He's got to be freezing his keester out there."

The guy looks out at the truck. It's a dim morning, one of those days when it never gets any brighter than it was just after dawn. And then he looks back at me, but he still doesn't speak. I'm starting to think he's one of those monks who took a vow of silence. But then he says, "You're right. OK." It's more of a croak than a speech— like those four syllables cost him a lot. But he puts down his crummy laundry and goes out to get the dog. Thank

God he also turns off the engine, I really don't want to
lecture him about that. Well, OK, actually I kinda do, but
I know better. The customer is always right. Almost.

He brings in the dog, with no leash, and that's fine, I
don't like leashes either, in spite of the laws these days.
Besides, this dog isn't going to take off on a mad dash
around the shop. I mean, this is an *old* dog. He's a black
lab, maybe with some hound in him, with a white muzzle
and milky eyes, and these are definitely his last legs. He
lurches on my slick linoleum floor—Roweena always
mops it after closing, you've got to have a clean floor in
this business—and his claws click as he catches himself,
trying to stay upright. But only for a few seconds. As soon
as the man turns back to his sorting, the dog goes under
the table and folds up like an accordion, whump, on the
floor. He looks sweet, like the kind of old guy you can
trust with all your secrets. But he is not in good shape.

I get him some water, in an old cereal bowl. I know
this man doesn't want my help; he really wants this to
be one of those automats where you don't have to deal
with anybody, just machines to dole out the tokens and
those nasty little packets of detergent—but I don't care.
This dog looks parched. I set the bowl by his head, and I
say "There you go, boy." What else should I say? "Cold
enough for you?" The dog eyes me warily—or eyes my
direction: it looks like maybe he's not seeing much anymore. The man looks down from the table and dredges
up a muttered "Thanks."

Carl always kept a dog or three for hunting, and I never

thought I'd say this, but I miss them. I mean, those dogs were smelly and expensive, and housetraining them was a pain, and our little yard was like a minefield, because Carl could not be bothered to clean up after them. He said my nose was too sensitive, and he was right about that—I can smell shit at a hundred paces. But Jessie loved those dogs, and they doted on her. The last three we had were Lola, Dixie, and Achilles, and they were all sweet-hearts. People think pit bulls are scary, but they never met Achilles. I used to call him Killer, just to freak people out. When we put Jessie out in the play pen, just to get some fresh air, he would stand guard by the hour, and when she was big enough, they romped like puppies. You know that T-shirt that says "Be The Person Your Dog Thinks You Are"? That's not bad advice.

I'd like to stay there and take care of the dog; I'd like to bring him some kibble, if only I had any; I'd like to learn his name. But you have to know your customers. This guy doesn't want to be in my debt. It's a sad way to be, but I'm not going to change it in a magical ninety minutes at the All-Kleen. So what can I do?

I can go back to the office and watch Linda Hamilton kick butt. Or I can work on Mrs. Hosper's weekly drop-off order from yesterday. Ever since she turned their guest room into an Airbnb, she goes through a ton of sheets. I washed them all yesterday, but I like to leave the folding until Sunday morning. I run them through the dryer one more time, so they're warm and ready for folding, and I lay her old blankets over a rack to make sure they're extra dry. Mildew can be brutal.

By now the guy has chucked his stuff into an all-purpose washer and tossed some cut-rate powder in with it. Stains, fading, ring around the collar? Oh well, sailor vee, as my mother used to say. He has discovered the free coffee stand and helped himself to a steaming cardboard cup, and also a slice of the coffee cake I always set out there in the morning. It's a good thing I didn't have to burden him by offering it. He has settled into the plastic chair next to his washer, and he's reading a *Picket Fence Preview* from the rack by the door. Is he looking to settle? Or just desperate to avoid conversation? I do him a favor and retire to the office.

One reason I love "The Terminator" is that I can root for both sides. I mean, you have to feel for Sarah Connor: she's just a waitress trying to make it through the day, and she's so pretty, and out of nowhere this psycho with a shotgun starts stalking her. Oh, and she's also going to be the mother of the savior of mankind. But I have to admit, part of me always roots for Arnold, too. I know I shouldn't call him that—he's the Terminator, the T800, Arnold is just the actor's name. But really? That guy is Ahnuld through and through. And he is so badass. The shades. The ratty clothes he stole from that punk kid. The wires in his wrists. The way he never cracks a smile. And he seems so *lonely*. I mean, he's the only cyborg on earth, and he's just trying to do his job.

When it's over, and Arnold has been crushed once again (but don't worry, he's a T800, you can't get rid of him that easily, you know there has to be a sequel), I look out and see that the man is still sitting quietly as his dryer turns, so I go downstairs to take care of my plants. I keep a garden all year round, and up here in Zone 4 that means some serious indoor gardening. You can grow almost anything year-round in containers, if you've got the right lights and enough space. It used to make Carl crazy that every year more of the house was taken up with plants and grow-lights — but as long as I didn't touch his man-cave, he let me be. After a while, I just ran out of room. But then I thought of the basement at the All-Kleen. It's just an unfinished space, long and narrow like the up-stairs, with a cement floor and cinderblock walls. There's an old metal slop sink, and an industrial-strength hot-wa-ter heater, and of course all the pipes for the washers up-stairs. Over the years I had just let stuff accumulate down there. But then I cleared out some space, and hauled a bunch of potted plants from the house, and set up some new grow-lights. It was ideal, warm and humid like the fern greenhouse in Montreal. I wasn't in Carl's way, and I could duck down there before opening the laundromat, or at the end of my shift, to check on my babies. At first I thought I was going to transplant everything in the spring, but then Carl died that winter, and I just left it all downstairs. Dee says, "Don't you want to get out in the fresh air?" Dee's into self-improvement. Me, I'm into kale and chard and runner beans. You can get dirt under your nails indoors or out.

It takes a good ten minutes to water everything, and

when I come back upstairs to the door on the back side of the office, there's the dog guy, standing at the half-door, peering in to my work space.

"Can I help you?" I ask.

He looks a little spooked, but he just says no.

"Dog OK?" I know, it's a dumb question, but it's the right one: the guy almost smiles. I mean, it's more of a flinch, a David Janssen smile — but still.

I pretend to have some paperwork, and in a minute I hear the clatter of claws on linoleum, and the bell rings again, and the truck coughs to a start outside. I go out to survey the damage. I figure this guy will have spilled some powder, or at the least one of the rolling baskets will need to be put back by the door. But no: the floor is clean and dry, there's no dog hair under the table, not an item out of place. But then I notice: the whole coffee cake is gone. What the hell. Well, I guess he liked it. I hope the dog got some.

Carl said we never should have let Jessie go off to Lyndon State. He and I never went to college, and we turned out all right. He said college was where she started liking girls. I said you don't know that, she could have found a girl around here. And he said, "Well, she didn't, did she?"

I was just glad if she found *some*body. I'm sorry I never said that. But what good would it have done? Children leave, that's their job. Why would they stay in a place like Lunenburg? I left *my* parents, back when I was pregnant with her. Still, I thought she'd come back to visit. She must have thought her father would eat her alive. Maybe she was right. He loved that girl so much.

The doctor said he was a good candidate for a stroke — a big guy who ate the wrong things and didn't exercise anymore. I tried to help, but habits are hard to change. One good thing: it was sudden.

Five days later, the dog guy comes in again. Being a Friday afternoon, it's busy: a lot of people like to do their laundry for the weekend. I've just got twenty washers and ten dryers, that's all we could fit in this skinny space. And usually it's enough. But on a Friday afternoon, when somebody steps out for a cup of coffee while their stuff is still in the dryer, and then their dryer finishes and somebody else is waiting with a basket full of wet clothes, well, things can get chippy. That's why I provide the coffee here for free, so people won't walk out. And I put up the sign saying "Do Not Leave The Premises While Your Load Is Drying." But do people read signs? Not in my experience.

So I always work a long shift on Fridays, doubling up with Roweena. And I'm always busy, making sure the token machine stays loaded, punching those ridiculous punch-cards that Carl suggested we institute, because there's nothing people like better than getting a free wash after they've done twenty. Really? You've carried that spindly bit of cardboard in your wallet for four months, just so you can save two bucks? No, I'm sorry, I cannot give you punches for the four times you swear you did washes but didn't happen to have the card with you; the card is your magic ticket.

Anyway, I'm so busy on this Friday afternoon that I don't even notice when the guy first comes in. I mean, the bell over the door gets pretty constant at those times, and I can't always look up. But then I hear a different set of chimes — the jingle of dog tags. And there's my old guy settling in under the sorting table where he was the other day. And he's looking even worse than before, a bag of bones in a mangy black pelt. Even with all the detergent in the air, I can tell he's not smelling so good. Let's just say he's not the kind of dog you want to pet. So of course I just feel for him more. I wonder why the guy would be back again so soon; he seems more like the once-a-month type. But sometimes people come in just because it's warm and full of activity, and that's OK with me. A good laundromat is like a community center. Everybody knows the All-Kleen has the best bulletin board around. Lunenburg is not a Craigslist kind of town.

Just when I'm about to get the dog a bowl of water, Filly Bonnefoy roars over to me, shouting "Peggy! Somebody pulled my clothes out of the dryer and dumped them in a basket, and they weren't even close to dry!" Filly has these tight little blond curls framing her face; she gets them done every week at Carolyn's House of Style. When she's agitated, they shake like a fringe of leaves.

I say, "I'm sorry, Filly, but did you, um, leave the premises?" Pointing to the sign.

And she says, "Well, I had to pick up some groceries! I am not one of these people who can afford to wait around all afternoon!" And I know what she means, because Serge Bonnefoy will damn sure want his dinner on the table when he gets home from his job over in Saint Johnsbury. But what can I do? We've got our rules. You leave, you lose. I offer Filly an extra punch on a new card, and she settles down. It's OK, because I know she's going to lose that card within days.

When I finally get around to remembering the bowl of water, I look over to the sorting table and I see that the dog is gone. I never even really saw the man this time, though I had the feeling of his presence, somewhere on the edge of my busyness. But I don't have any time to think about it, because here's Filly Bonnefoy in my face again, after she has finally finished her stupid drying and folded up her stuff. Her ringlets are bouncing against her temples, and she's shouting, "Peggy! One of my shirts is missing!"

I say, "Are you sure, Filly?"

And she glares. "You think I don't know my own laundry? I know I put three of Serge's flannel shirts in that washer, because it's all the flannel shirts he's got, and he wears them all the time, and that's why they always need washing! And now there are just two! Whoever removed my things from that dryer obviously helped themselves to one of those shirts! The red one with the black plaid!" And she looks around the All-Kleen accusatorily.

"Well, that's terrible, Filly. Maybe that person just made

a mistake, you know, there are a lot of those shirts in circulation. You could put a Lost and Found note on the board."

Filly is not mollified. She's fuming about how she can take her business elsewhere. I give her another punch, and that helps a little. She and I both know that she will be back next week. Maybe next time she won't leave the premises.

The next day after work, I'm at The Regulator, the only bar in Lunenburg, just across the street. It's my Saturday beer with the Merry Widows, and we're talking about this sci-fi movie Rastus saw last week. I don't get out to new movies anymore, so I count on Rastus to keep me updated. He used to teach art down at Lyndon State, and he's got a good eye. It was his idea to call us "the Merry Widows." He says "widower" is a weird word. Since Molly died, movies are his favorite thing; he says he can lose himself there. I'm just the opposite: going to the movies alone just makes me sad.

Rastus says this new movie is well made and all, but he just cannot buy the time-travel stuff. "Time only moves in one direction," he says. "Just ask my knees." Rastus used to be a damn good athlete—he was the point guard on our high school team, and his job was to feed the ball to Carl, the big man in the post. Even in high school, when Carl and I were just dating, Rastus always called me The Giant's Wife. He still works out, and he's still got most of his hair, gone to silver and curling over his ears.

Dee says, "I can time-travel."

Dee looks like Angelina Jolie, if you can imagine a small-town, 65-year-old version. After Jerry died, she got a little heavier, but I swear, she could still take out a battalion of bad guys with those cheekbones. She is also a B. S. artist from way back.

She says, "Aren't you going to ask me how?"

Rastus says, "Why ask? We know you're going to tell us anyway."

"All right, wise guy. Watch."

We watch. She sits there. We watch some more. She takes a sip of her beer. The cash register beeps, cutlery clinks, the ceiling fan makes a whooshing swoop, then another. The white Christmas lights outside the window blink on and off a few times in the early dark. Dee looks at her watch and smiles.

"Very funny," I say.

"There's only one way to stop time," she says. "And I'm not signing up."

Rastus laughs his good-sport laugh. You have to indulge Dee, if you want her company. I tell them about Arnold going back in time to snuff out the as-yet unimpregnated mother-to-be of the man who will save humanity from the apocalypse. This is after two beers, but before three.

Dee breaks into a big Cher voice. "If I could turn back ti-ime . . ."

Rastus says, "You can't do that. It's like going back and killing your own grandfather. You'd never be born. So how could you go back and kill him?"

And I say, "But Arnold wasn't born, he was made! He's a T800! He can go back and kill anybody he wants! Dee, stop caterwauling! Who wants another beer?" That shuts her up.

That night, I'm already in my home clothes — an old sweat suit from when I was still a jogger — when I get a call from Roweena.

"Aunt Peggy?"

I'm not her aunt, but I've known her since she was in swaddling clothes. Her voice is hushed; I can barely hear it over the boomity music from the radio she always plays in the office. "There's this guy in the shop?" Roweena makes everything sound like a question.

"What guy?" I'm a little slow after that third beer.

"This guy with a dog?"

The beer fizzles from my system. "Yeah, what about him?"

"He's kinda freaking me out?"

"What's he doing?"

"Well, I was busy in the front, you know, that dryer that keeps cutting out after five minutes? This customer was complaining, and I kept going out to help, you know, you just have to jiggle the handle the right way?"

"I know, I have to call the service rep. But the guy with the dog?"

"Well, when I got back to the office, he was in here?"

"In the office? Doing what?"

"I don't know? I mean, he was, like, looking around?

When he saw me, he asked if I had some water for his dog? So I got him some, because this dog, he doesn't look so good? And the guy went back out to the front table, you know" — she's whispering — "but he doesn't even have any laundry with him? He's just, like, sitting there?"

"I'll be right there," I say, and I throw on my long down coat. By the time I get there, the truck is gone, and so is the man with the dog. I help Roweena close up. There's nothing missing from the office, but when I get home, I lie awake a long time.

"Hooskelah, hooskelah," Carl used to say. It didn't mean anything; it was just this little nonsense thing he said to himself when he thought no one was listening. Sometimes these days I say it myself. It feels good in your mouth.

A week later, the man with the dog comes into the All-Kleen again. It's the week before Christmas, a Saturday morning, when things are pretty slow, so I get a good look at him. He doesn't have any laundry; he just goes straight to the bulletin board and posts a note of some kind. And damned if underneath that flimsy tan coat he's not wearing a red flannel shirt with black plaid. But like I said, there are a lot of those shirts around, so I don't say anything.

Until I see the dog, which didn't follow him across the room; it just collapsed by the door. When the man finishes at the bulletin board, he goes back over there and starts to get the dog up. But it doesn't want to move. The man pulls it up on its matchstick legs, and the dog starts making these little yips. I remember those yips. That was when the vet said we had to put Achilles down.

The man keeps trying to get the dog on its feet, and the dog keeps refusing. Or failing. He reaches under the dog's rump for a new grip, and the dog summons up some energy and snaps at his hand, and the man swears, and gives it a swat on the snout. Not hard — but still. I'm over there before I even realize I'm walking.

"I'll call a vet," I say.

The man looks up at me, holding his hand. It's not bleeding. His eyes are hard. "How is this your business?"

"Your dog needs help!"

"It's my dog."

"And it's my shop! I can call someone if I want to."

He sets his mouth, like there's more he wants to say. But he doesn't say it. I hurry to the office to get my phone, and I call the Pet Emergency number outside of Saint J. The woman says to bring the animal in. I say we'll be there in twenty minutes. I grab my coat. And when I get back to the front door, the man and the dog are gone. So is the truck.

On the bulletin board there's a new index card, with a neatly lettered note in ballpoint. "Handyman Seeks Work. No Job Too Large or Small. Call Jack," with a phone number.

The Merry Widows are divided. Dee says I should call the cops. Rastus says, "Every man in this county has one of those shirts. Did Filly sew Serge's name in it?"

I say, "You know Filly wouldn't be caught dead with a needle and thread."

Dee says, "The man was hitting his dog in a public place!"

Rastus says, "And what law does that break?"

It's another three-beer evening.

And the next day is Sunday. Good morning, big guy. I hope there are football games on TV in heaven.

Driving in to the All-Kleen, I see the green truck parked at the Rite Aid, which is open 24-7, even on Sunday. I figure the man — Jack — has a right to park where he wants. But I stop anyway, walk to the truck, and hunch over at the passenger-side window. If he's left that dog out in this cold . . . But no, there's no dog in the cab. So I go into the Rite Aid, and I walk every aisle. Lots of Christmas tinsel, but no man or dog. And then I know. Or let's just say I get this feeling.

I drive to the All-Kleen, and park in the little lot behind it, where there's an outside door that leads into the back hall and the steps down to the basement. The door is unlocked. Did I leave it open? Carl always insisted on locking every-thing. I said, "It's Lunenburg, Vermont! Who's going to rob us?" And he said, "You don't want to borrow trouble."

I take the steps quietly. Downstairs, the grow lights are glowing, as usual. Everything looks normal — plants and boxes and old equipment I should have got rid of long ago. But I can smell it. The musky smell of a pelt that hasn't been washed in months.

He wouldn't.

I follow my nose. In the darkest corner, I see a box turned on its side, with the bottom pushed out, and inside it a lumpy form, under one of Mrs. Hosper's blankets. I hadn't even missed it.

The lump doesn't stir. And then it does stir, ever so slightly, in the rhythm of a breathing sleeper. And it's too big for just one skinny dog. It's both of them, sleeping in my basement.

What am I supposed to do? I want to shout, I want to call the cops, I want to call a vet. What would Sarah Connor do?

I go quietly upstairs. It's 6:35. I have to open the laundromat.

It's a moderately busy day, for a Sunday—people getting ready for Christmas parties, I guess. One guy even brings in a Santa suit. You know that thing needs dry cleaning—but if this guy wants to ruin his costume in a heavy-duty washer, I am not one to turn away business. The truth is, my mind is downstairs. But I do not want to go down there.

When Rowena finally comes in for her shift, late as usual, I have no choice. Well, all right, I have a choice. I choose to go downstairs. And the guy is awake this time.

He's standing by the slop sink, which is full of water and the saddest looking dog you ever saw. It was already scrawny; in the water, it's a black pipe-cleaner, twisted in impossible shapes.

The man doesn't look surprised or guilty. He doesn't look anything, just neutral. Like he does this every day. His voice is flat.

"I thought a bath would help."

The dog is making little whimpering noises. The man says, "It's OK, Joe." To me he says, "He's just cold." He drains the water from the sink and reaches for a towel he must have borrowed on one of his visits upstairs.

I say, "You can't do this."

"I'll have him out of the sink in no time." Again that flat voice.

"No, you can't *do* this," I say, with a spastic sweep of my arm that takes in the whole basement.

"Yes, I can," he says. "I *am* doing this."

He is so focused on his task — drying this dog named Joe — that he can't see anything else.

I have seen this look before. Carl, when Jessie left.

"I've got to go," I say. "Dry off your dog."

And I leave. But I don't sleep much that night.

Dog food
Old blankets
Plastic bags
Call vet
Syringe?

The next morning, I go in early. The truck isn't at the Rite Aid, or at the All-Kleen, either. But when I get downstairs, the dog is there, under the blanket. Still breathing.

Maybe Jack went out for food.

There's only one thing to do. I leave the "Closed" sign facing out on the front door.

When I get back from the vet's, Jack is waiting, outside his truck. The Christmas lights at the Regulator are blinking faintly in the wan morning sun. It's too cold to be standing outside. His breath plumes above him. He still doesn't have a hat.

I get out of the Subaru and go to the hatchback. I pick up the bundle as gently as I can. A clean white blanket. I cradle it in my arms and walk towards Jack.

I hold it out to him, and he just has to open his arms for it. A chickadee makes its two-note call.

Jack doesn't say anything. What's he going to do, thank me? I don't want to be thanked. When I hand it to him, he just stares at it. He didn't want this. Neither did I. But I would do it again.

I imagine him bedding down in his box tonight, under Mrs. Hosper's blanket, in the warm basement of the All-Kleen. He doesn't know how tired he is. He is like Adam discovering sleep. When he wakes up, he will think, What is this? And the answer will be: Today.

Vote No to Say Yes

All I ever wanted for her was everything. After the misery of her birth, I knew she was going to be my only child, no matter what Mac said about wanting more. The labor was like something out of a nineteenth-century novel. I caterwauled, I crawled, I careened around our living room, where Evie and I had put down newspaper to protect the floor. After ten hours of agony, the midwife said, "Ruth, maybe a Caesarean would be best, after all." Evie nodded. She had come from across the street, a compact ball of energy, ready to help with anything. And Mac? He was at the door to the front hall, cell phone in hand, primed to call 911. But I was going to bring this child into the world as women had done for centuries. When did we decide that life was supposed to be pain-free?

Finally, Harper arrived, a little misshapen mucus-head, screaming like a Jewish banshee. I was screaming, too. It seems right, now, that shrieking ushered her into the world.

After that, well, Mac didn't need to know that I was

on the pill. He gave me a sideways look sometimes, and I felt bad about it — but we were busy, we had a healthy baby, we didn't need to tempt fate by trying for another. I was an only child myself, and I always thought, why would my parents have wanted more? Wasn't I enough?

Harper was enough for me. But from the start, there was just no pleasing her. God knows I tried. I pumped my breasts until they were sore, closing my office door on the students racketing down the hall — and she always wanted more. Aren't babies supposed to get full and drop off into stupefied sleep? Not Harper. Oh, she must have slept sometimes, or she never would have grown into such a beanpole — but that's not what I remember. What I remember is a mouth howling for more.

I was glad the birth happened in the summer, so I could get right back to my classes in the fall, with day care at the little center down the street. I wanted Harper to start getting socialized. And I couldn't leave my work unattended, even for a semester. Mac assured me that the world could go on without me for a few months. But no one else was ready to take the lead on the new Environmental Studies major, or the Clean Campus Contract, or the campaign to fund neighborhood gardens around Burlington. It was the start of a new century, and the whole movement was just beginning to gather momentum. If someone didn't push it ahead right then, it could fall back and dissipate, maybe never get moving again. I wanted Harper to see a mother who was a full-time person in the world, making it a better place. I wanted her never to doubt that a girl can do whatever she wants. All I ever wanted for her was everything.

Her early years are a blur to me now. Mac and I managed, but it was an awkward dance. Sometimes it felt like one of us had to be The Good Guy and one had to be The Monster. Guess which I was. But what was I supposed to do? There was Mac, sneaking Skittles into her room after we had agreed that the house would be sugar-free, or letting her watch videos on his office computer even though we had said she shouldn't have any screen time until she was older. I know he just wanted her to be happy. But how could he be so weak? When she was crying, he wilted.

And she certainly knew how to cry. When I tried to apply the rules, I felt like the Ogress of a fairy tale, the one who eats little children with a sauce Robert. I know Harper loved him more. How could she not? But that wasn't the kind of love a parent should want. I was being punished for being the only grownup in the house.

When I confronted him about it, Mac said, "You're right, sweetie, I should be tougher." And then he retreated into his study to read those ridiculous books about expeditions to the South Pole, Scott and Shackleton and all that epic waste of energy. After a few days, Harper was clawing at his door for the attention that had been wrenched away from her. I'd try to get her focused on some craft project at the kitchen table, so I could keep up with my e-mail or grade papers while she puttered away—but puttering was not Harper's M.O. She could never believe she was getting it right, even if I insisted there was no such thing as "right." I should have known better. I can still hear my own mother saying, "There is always a best way, Ruthie; you just have to find it." Even as a little girl, I respected that.

I want to be fair: Mac did his part. He was always an early riser, so he could get Harper up in the morning, which wasn't easy, because she never wanted to sleep at night. He pried her out of bed and made her eat some cereal, although she only ever wanted Pop-Tarts. Then he got her off to school, where she never wanted to go. And he was there at the end of the day, too, because his 9-to-5 at the library was really more like 10-to-4. His supervisor was one of his drinking buddies. So if I had a committee meeting or a rally in town, Mac could fix dinner. Harper always liked his eleven variations on mac 'n' cheese better than my veggie medleys, anyway. For a while he called her Cheese-Head, so the two of them, of course, were Mac and Cheese. But mostly he called her Beansprout. She was always tall for her age, a hank of yellow hair on a body outgrowing its clothes.

I called her Harper. Give a person a name, I thought, and honor it.

If I had been softer, would she still be here now? But if I had been softer, I would not have been me.

We were doing important things in those years. That was when we got the Barge Canal cleaned up, so the lake wouldn't be poisoned by toxic sludge. We extended the bike path, after fighting for months to win right-of-way from those pig-headed property owners who wanted to preserve their private access to the lake. The land belongs to all of us! What better lesson could there be for Harper? And we put so much heat on that gun manufacturer in Lakeside that they finally moved out of town, lock, stock, and both barrels. People said it was manipulative to put my child on the picket line, holding a sign that said "No Tools of Death in My City!" But Harper was completely on board with that: she helped make the sign, and she carried it proudly. I don't think we ever had a better day.

Before she was born, Mac had wanted to live in the country, where his precious Sloppy Joe could romp without a leash and our children could grow up surrounded by birds and squirrels. "Why live in Vermont," he said, "if you're just going to be in a town? You could do that anywhere."

We were at the kitchen table of that ratty place on Murray Street, our first apartment, with the fluorescent light buzzing overhead and the linoleum peeling below. I knew Mac had a point.

"But a child would just feel isolated out there," I said. "She'd depend even more than most kids on phones and computers to keep in touch, and we'd be driving her endlessly to soccer practice and music lessons."

"'Her'?" Mac said. "Do you know something I don't know?"

"No!" I laughed. "I just have this feeling."

We fell silent, and I swear something else entered the

room. Off to the side, by the window that looked out on a slushy street in the early dark of February. I'm not prone to mystic visions, but I felt that something was appraising us.

I said, "We need to commit ourselves to our community. Town life is the best way to live sustainably now, to leave the smallest footprint. When we get our own place, we'll have a garden, grow a lot of our own food, preserve and can things for winter. We won't have to drive ten miles to the nearest Stop 'n' Rob."

Mac laughed. "You're going into Lecture Mode, sweetie. But OK, I get it. I'm gonna be the most sustainable guy you ever knew. Let's get us a house in town."

And before long we bought the house on Louise Street where Harper was born. Such a sweet little neighborhood, a mile from downtown, with small yards where people put Adirondack chairs and wading pools. Evie and Leah were the perfect neighbors, right across the street. And it wasn't like Mac gave up everything. He kept that old eyesore of a truck, and every November he took off for a hunting trip with Hooley and Skiff, those guys he grew up with in Bristol. They drove God knows where, and slept on the frosty ground, ate chili from cans, and drank vats of beer. He came back scruffy and achy from squatting in a hunting blind all week, and just so pleased with himself for having a life out there in the woods, a life I didn't share. He always took Sloppy Joe, and Harper pined for them both, and talked about how she'd go hunting when she grew up. Of course, I wanted her to do whatever she wanted, and to break down gender stereotypes along the way — but I wasn't so keen on killing woodland animals. "What about the tools of death?" I said. She just looked at me funny.

So we got used to our little life in the city. I was so busy with my classes and our projects in town that I probably wasn't as present as I could have been for Mac and Harper. But they were busy, too. Mac seemed to like his work well enough, but I always had the feeling that it wasn't what he really wanted. Or maybe I just wanted more for him. That was one of the things that worried my parents: he was so low-key, he didn't seem to have any dreams. Once, before we were married, my father asked him, straight up, "What do you want to do with your life?"

I winced. We were sitting on the little deck at Murray Street on a gorgeous autumn afternoon, sunlight bright on Daddy's well-tanned skull. My father was making his annual visit from New Your, back when he still bothered. My father the neurologist liked asking direct questions.

Mac pointed his beer can at the deck, and also at the light sluicing through the silver maple. "I'm doing it, Don. I want to sit on a deck with a beer, and go hunting, and follow the Red Sox. And raise a family, eventually," he added, though we hadn't talked about that yet. "Some people live to work," he said. "I work to live."

My father looked at me. I said, "Who needs another beer?"

One Sunday morning when Harper was five or six, she and I were in the family room of the house on Louise Street. I had *The New York Times* scattered everywhere, just the way I like it; she was working on a coloring book, drawing madly outside the lines. I don't know where Mac was—maybe one of those hunting trips. The classical music station was on, as usual, playing early music, Gregorian chant and plainsong. I've never been a church or temple person, but that music seemed right for Sunday morning, human voices at their most divine.

The announcer told us about the piece we were about to hear, which featured the refrain, "Parfaitement, sans oblier." Her mention of the title reminded me of something I'd learned in college French—that in traditional verse, the silent "e" gets pronounced, so it was "parfaitement," in four syllables. I loved that. And "oblier," of course, was an old spelling for "oublier," to forget. But the translation she offered was better: "Perfectly, and without fail."

When did things start to go wrong? I look back now at moments that seemed like normal little family problems, and I wonder, Was that it? I don't want to blame it on Harper. But the phase when she stopped sleeping was hard.

She was eight or nine at the time. Every night, she hung around the kitchen past her bedtime, claiming she wasn't sleepy, even though her eyelids were drooping. Every night, while I got some work done in my study,

Mac tucked her in and told her a story. And every night, hours later, she appeared at our room, back when we still shared a room, wanting us to keep her company. I say "us," but she didn't want me. She wanted to climb into bed on Mac's side, she wanted another story. We started calling this "badtime."

Mostly, Mac dealt with it. He walked her back to her room, and he told her stories until she fell asleep. Sometimes, in the morning, as she poured her Cheerios, spilling more than she ate, I got to hear the residue.

"So this guy tried to walk all the way across Anarchica, pulling this big sled with all his food and stuff. He didn't even have a sled dog! He wanted to do it alone."

"Antarctica?"

"Maybe. Yeah. You know, the South Pole? Where the penguins live? Only he didn't see any penguins, I don't know why. Maybe it was too cold for them. But this guy just kept going, no matter how cold it got. He had tried once before, with a couple of friends, but they had to turn back, because one of the other guys got frostbite and they had to cut his nose off. Anyway, he wanted to do it alone, to impress the Queen."

"So did he make it?"

She looked out the window, big hazel eyes searching the back yard for an answer. "I guess I fell asleep."

It was like listening to someone recount her dreams. At least she slept, so score one for Mac. I think he actually thrived on those nights. Getting Harper to sleep was something he could fix, one night at a time.

And I hated him for that. I was losing our daughter, and he was winning. I know it wasn't a competition. But still.

I don't think it was the cancer that did us in. I mean, yes, it was hard—but of course Mac was supportive, and we tried not to let it bother Harper. She was twelve at the time, and being a human adolescent is hard enough without watching your mother deal with a lethal disease. I told her I had a lump in my breast, and they were going to take it out, and then I would get better. I said it was like kids who need orthodontia. They get their braces, and it's a pain, but they live with it, no big deal. She didn't need to know about radiation and chemo, and those ridiculous hospital gowns with the back flapping open just in case you didn't already feel like your insides have been laid out on a public grill. What else should I have told her? I didn't know how I felt about it myself.

I remember sitting in the Oncology waiting room, where I spent so much time in those days—rows of chairs under fluorescent lights; pamphlets in plastic racks on the walls, touting recovery groups; a whiteboard featuring magnetic poetry, where you could arrange words like "hope" and "courage" in cheerful constellations. It was my first day of chemo, and I was scared out of my mind. I had told Mac that I wanted to do this alone. He protested, but he could tell I wasn't going to change my mind. It takes a certain graciousness to accept help when you're vulnerable. I didn't have it then.

Several chairs down, a couple of women were chatting,

as if they were at the laundromat waiting for the spin cycle to end.

"My body is a road map," one of them said. She was a tall, elegant woman in her fifties, wearing a pink head wrap. "My body is one big scar."

The other woman was smaller, more condensed; she reminded me of Evie, whom I hadn't told yet about my trouble. She was scrolling through stuff on her tablet. She glanced up and said, "Preach!"

And the tall woman preached. "I used to have pretty feet," she said. "You know? It's not so much to brag about — but they were nice feet. Dainty. I painted my toe-nails." She laughed at the very idea. "Aubergine, that was my shade."

"Uh-huh," the shorter woman said. "I like aubergine."

"Now, thanks to all the stuff they pump into me here, my feet are yellow and bloated, and my toenails are fall-ing out." She was practically singing. "My old shoes don't fit no more."

"Oh, honey," said her friend.

"Now I don't have pretty anything."

"Oh, you're doing fine, sweetie. Don't talk yourself down."

"I had to go out and get a whole new collection of shoes."

"Ha!"

"So at least there's that," the tall woman said, and they laughed.

I listened to that, and I thought, how can they laugh? I wanted to riff like that on my disaster.

I have to say, Mac was great, all that time. It can't have been easy for him. He was still the wash-and-wear guy he had always been, like "wake me up and give me a cup of coffee and I'll deal with the day." And here was his wife, freaked out not because of the cancer itself but because she might have to abandon some of her work. He tried to persuade me to focus on myself for a while—and of course that was right, but could I do it? We were just getting started on our biggest project yet—fighting City Place, that behemoth mix of luxury condos and chain stores, which would change our downtown for decades to come.

Mac said, "And if it does? Will the world end?"

And I said, "The world will be worse. Harper's Burlington will be a corporate playground where ordinary people can't live."

He said, "What makes you think Harper will want to stay in this little provincial town?" Maybe he already knew what she would do. Or maybe he just wanted to hurt me a little, as payback for not letting him come with me to treatments. But he took care of the grocery shopping and the laundry and the cooking. He set his mouth in that thin line.

And then I gained all that weight. This was a special shame to me, hard to talk about even now. All my life I had been a skinny girl, and proud of it—a careful eater who made sure to get her exercise. In high school, I was borderline anorexic, and my parents cheered me on. They wouldn't have admitted this, but I'm sure they believed that being thin was Step One in catching a man. And they weren't entirely wrong. Mac always praised my slimness. I don't think he would have gone for a big woman.

After the treatments, though, something had to give. It's not like I told myself, "OK, Ruthie, time to get fat!" But my body had a mind of its own. For months, there had been so many things I couldn't eat—nothing spicy, nothing rich, nothing greasy, no tomato-based sauces. When I got through the radiation and the chemo and I could eat again, I started eating like I might never get another chance. It was like I was pregnant again. I just wanted home fries with lots of onions and garlic, burritos with salsa and guacamole and heaps of sour cream. And did I mention guacamole? I slipped out of the house early, saying I had to get to work—which was nothing new, I had always been early to the grind—and I arrived at Sneakers just as they were opening, so I could stake out the back corner booth, with my back to the door, and savor my home fries in peace. Washed down with bottomless cups of cream-laden coffee, it was heaven on a plate.

Of course, my hips ballooned. I took it as an occasion to buy new underwear, new outfits, shapeless but colorful tents that would accommodate the new Ruth. I put on a couple new chins, and told myself this was an improvement; I had always been a chinless wonder. Even my fingers gained weight. I had to screw off several rings because they were starting to cut off the circulation.

And Mac never said boo. During the treatments, we

had started sleeping in separate rooms, at my suggestion, because I was often so exhausted that I collapsed into bed by 7:00, and then I was up several times in the night, retching into the kitchen sink or fixing myself some hot milk that I wouldn't be able to swallow. So our sex life had evaporated, anyway. When the treatments were over, we just kept it that way. We both liked having room for our own stuff, our own habits. He could stay up watching some stupid ballgame from the west coast, eat Cheez-Doodles in bed, and snore to his heart's delight. I could wear an extra-large T-shirt to bed, and get up early to slip out for my home fries tryst. I thought Mac didn't care anymore; I thought maybe he had found something on the side, and the truth was I didn't want to know. I thought the less said the better.

But dealing with Harper was more difficult. It's not like we had ever been girly-girls together, chattering over dress racks. I wanted her to find her own style, and No Style was always an option. When I was in my Elephant Woman phase, she was sporting black T-shirts. And they looked good against her golden hair.

One of those nights, I was in the kitchen, tucking into a midnight snack—a roast chicken from Shaw's, the whole bird laid out on its plastic tray, greasy and delicious. I must have decided it would be too long until Sneakers opened. At the hallway door I heard a small noise, and there she was, just looking at me. By then, at age twelve, she had heard enough of her mother in Lecture Mode to know that a chain-store chicken is just about the lowest rung on the ladder of conscious eating. It's raised in a cage with a floor the size of a sheet of notebook paper; it stands in its own excrement, unable to walk; and it's fed with corn products to create an unnaturally large breast, then with antibiotics to ward off the ravages of such conditions. The corn comes from fields that once were forests, providing oxygen to us and homes to birds. So my moment at the kitchen table was not only hip-padding and artery-clogging, but cruel and planet-destroying. And of course I knew all of this; I just couldn't stop myself.

Standing at the door, Harper didn't comment. She just said, "Hi, Mom." Then she turned and went upstairs.

The chicken glistened on its plastic platter. I took another bite.

The cancer subsided. It didn't go away; the doctor said it almost certainly wouldn't. I would have to do scans for the rest of my life. But for now, she said, it was in abeyance. Strange word, *abeyance*. It was at bay, the wolf at the door. We would do our best, she said, to keep that door secure. She was a hopeful sort.

Some people would have decided that now, having survived an assault, they should leave the exhaustion and anxiety of work behind. Evie brought a casserole across the street—as if I needed a casserole—and said, "Ruth, don't you see that the cancer came from all that stress? Can't you let someone else save the world?"

But I am not some people. Work is what I'm for. The campaign against City Place was underway. We had formed a group to fight it—a coalition of small business owners, advocates for affordable housing, and environmentalists, who foresaw that this massive thing would throw its shadow over several crucial blocks of our little city. The mayor was talking about "a new vision for Burlington," portraying us as obstructionists, lovers of the status quo. He backed a ballot initiative that asked voters to approve an exception to the city's limit on the height of structures, and also a spending bill that would use taxpayer money to pay the private developers, who would reap all the profit. It was outrageous.

I had been granted a reprieve, and I was going to use it on the front lines. Life is like money: it's no earthly good if you don't spend it.

Mac gave me that sideways look. But then he nodded. I could hear him thinking, right. This is the woman I married.

And Harper. It wasn't the cancer that drove her away. It was the recovery.

But first, Mac left. One morning when I got to the kitchen, I found a note on the counter, saying he just had to go. Now that I had recovered, he said, it was time for him to move on. Harper was old enough to start figuring out her own path, get out of his shadow. He said this was best for all of us.

He was taking the dog, and this was best, too, he said, because Sloppy was on his last legs. Mac would deal with the final phase, and spare us that sadness. I think he actually believed this.

He said he wasn't taking a phone or a credit card; he was going to make a fresh start.

Even in my bewilderment, I just had to smile. *Now?* I thought. Now he's getting some ambition? Well, good luck to him.

It was a wet Saturday morning in October. I checked his closet. The empty coat hangers dangled.

Harper was still in bed. There was a coalition meeting in town that day. I got back to work.

The fight over City Place dragged on. These things take years—that's part of what you learn when you're in this work. You have to play the long game. The mayor and the big-money people made their pitch, with PowerPoint slides of their glitzy new buildings and "environmental impact studies" written by hired hacks. We went to the courts for an injunction; we held public meetings that no one attended; we raised money to fund real environmental studies. And all the while, the political climate kept shifting, making it impossible to predict how the wind would blow when it came to a vote. There's so much you can't control. The Obama years were winding down, and the next presidential campaign was already in motion, that ridiculous crew of Republican candidates gathering like a murder of crows.

Finally, the vote was set for November of 2016. Just a month away now. And even the ballot is fixed against us: it's worded so that a "Yes" vote will approve the new development, the public funding, the vision of those private profiteers. So we're stuck with exactly the image the mayor wants: we're the "negative Nancies" — his not-so-subtle reminder to voters that most of our leaders are female. And we're left promoting a slogan that sounds like a contortionist's trick: "Vote NO to Say YES to a Livable City!"

I know I'm giving myself too much credit when I say that I drove Harper away. She had been leaving for years, ever since she discovered that doors open outwards. And she had been obsessed with that boy for months, sneaking out to meet him God knows where. Evie said she saw them hanging out in the park down the street, perched on the jungle gym, smoking. Evie knew I'd be disgusted by the smoking. Harper was only fifteen.

But that boy was just a vehicle. After her father left, it was only a matter of time. And what was I going to do? Lock her in her room? She would have let herself out the window on her long yellow hair.

The jungle gym is just down the hill from our community garden, which we helped create. On the refrigerator I keep a photograph that shows Harper and Mac in the summer of 2010, driving the final stake into the garden gate. Harper is all elbows and knees, wearing my floppy straw hat. They're both holding the big sledge hammer, mugging for the camera.

Parfaitement, sans oblier.

I know we're going to lose the ballot initiative. It's so hard to fight an incumbent mayor, and all those glossy plans. When I walk downtown, in the shadow of the towers they'll build, I can already feel a cold breeze. At least we'll have a woman in the White House.

Le Tourbillon

Paris, Ruth thinks, will be a test. Mac, snoring now beside her on the transatlantic flight, has never been there. Can he possibly appreciate it as she does—as the capital of the world, the cradle of civilized values, the dream city of her heart? Probably too much to ask. But she hopes he will get a glimpse of why she loves it so. She has planned every day of their week with walks in neighborhoods that matter to her, either because of particular memories or because of issues that engage her now. Part of this is nostalgia for her twenty-year-old self spending her junior year abroad: what was she nine years ago? And part of it is business: she has received a travel grant from the university, especially geared to help junior faculty get a start on their careers. The main question of her research: what makes a city sustainable? On the cusp of the twenty-first century, how is Paris doing?

She wishes she could pull her head away from Mac's shoulder, where it has been deposited for the past hour, but she doesn't want to wake him. They have never traveled together, except for day trips around Vermont—apple picking, minor hikes, a couple of visits to his brother on the family farm in Bristol. After living together for six months in Burlington, they know each other's quirks. But their jobs— he's a reference librarian, also at the university—keep them out of each other's hair. Here, they'll be together night and day. And Paris, she knows, intensifies everything.

Ruth has not told anyone that she thinks of their trip as a test. Not her parents, who, after a bitter divorce, have largely ignored their only child, as if she was a reminder of The Great Mistake. Not her new friends at the university, where she just started working last year. She knows it's not cool to turn such a trip into a trial. And certainly not Mac: that would just be embarrassing. She wants to emulate his low-key approach to everything. Wants it so much her stomach hurts.

Dawn arrives at Roissy, a muggy August morning on tarmac fields where massive planes burn lakes of fuel as they inch toward gates and runways. Ruth and Mac get on a shuttle that takes them to another shuttle that takes them to a waiting room where they get a bus that takes them to the Gare du Nord. Ruth had forgotten what the great train station is like: loud and crowded, littered and gritty, smelling of urine and sweat. At each new indignity along their path, she winces, looking over at Mac to see how he's taking it all. She wants to apologize: *this* isn't Paris, just wait. But he just smiles and focuses on the task at hand, shouldering his backpack and pulling their one shared bag.

Finally, they burst into the sunlight on the busy triangle in front of the station. Now, she thinks, now it begins.

It is a short walk to their lodging—a maid's room on the sixth floor of an ordinary apartment building on the busy little rue du Faubourg Poissonnière. Like many middle-class families, the people Ruth stayed with nine years ago own a *chambre de bonne* on a higher floor. The concierge, a sixtyish woman with a pale blue nylon pinafore over her house dress, comes out of her ground-floor office to accompany them. The last stop of the elevator is at the fifth floor; to reach the maids' floor you have to climb a narrow stair. The hallway is windowless, and lights up for just the sixty seconds before the *minuterie* shuts off its single bulb. It smells of cooking that must have been done on hot plates in other rooms along the mysterious hall. This is not *luxe* accommodation. But it's free. Although Ruth was never especially close to her French family, she played host to their teenaged daughter on a tour of New England, and now the favor is being returned. Her travel grant was meant for one, and she's intent on stretching it as far as it will go. Letting them in, the concierge tells Ruth they shouldn't expect to see the family—it's August, *vous savez?*—but she and her *petit ami* are welcome for the week.

Once they're alone, Ruth translates for Mac. She says she's too old to have a *petit ami*, but Mac says, "That's exactly what I am. I'm your little friend." He is a rangy guy with a thinning crown of rusty hair and a ruddy hawkish look. Ruth, much shorter, has wild dark hair that floats above the pale medallion of her face. Unpacking, he announces that he has brought a single pair of cargo pants to get him through the week. "It's 1999," he says. "Too late to fret about dress codes."

The room is spare. Two single beds, which they push together; a flimsy chiffonier for clothes; a scarred wooden table with two rickety chairs; and a single window that looks out over slate rooftops. It will offer cross-ventilation only if they open the door to the fetid hallway. Ruth hasn't planned for the heat; she has never been in Paris in the summer. But they won't be spending much time here: they have come to see the city, not to hole up in a room.

Her approach to jetlag, she has told Mac, is not to succumb to a nap on the first day, no matter how sleepy you are; that will just throw off your rhythms entirely. Instead, she says, you have to soldier through that day until a normal bedtime, get a regular night's sleep, and you'll be fine by Day Two.

They start with a walk up to Sacré-Coeur. It's just fifteen minutes from their room, and Ruth has figured that after their long, cramped night, the climb will be invigorating. But was it really this many steps nine years ago? Well, she wasn't jetlagged then. And it wasn't this hot. Catching her breath on a landing, she explains the origins of Montmartre.

"In the third century," she says, "This hill was well outside the city, and was a place of druidic worship. Paris was just a little Roman settlement at the time. When the

Romans decided to kill Denis, the leader of the city's Christians, they had him beheaded here, along with a couple of his followers. So the hill became known as le Mont des Martyrs, or Montmartre."

"Cool," says Mac, as he stretches his calves on one of the steps.

"Legend has it," Ruth adds, "that Denis then picked up his head and carried it on foot for several miles, preaching a sermon all the way. The spot where he eventually died, a little north of here, became the great basilica of Saint Denis."

Mac says, "Now there's a guy who didn't lose his head."

They get coffee at the Place du Tertre, which is already crawling with tourists. They are propositioned four times by sketch artists who want to draw cartoons of them for exorbitant fees. Mac sounds willing, but Ruth refuses to stoop to certain depths of tourist tackiness. As if in revenge, the coffee is undrinkable.

So she bundles them into the metro for a long ride to the sixteenth arrondissement. Abbesses, Pigalle, St. Georges, Notre Dame de Lorette, Trinité, St. Lazare . . . the stations they rattle through are all part of a comforting litany. But the subway seems louder and dirtier than she recalled it, and the passengers look absolutely zombified. Mac stands at one of the metal poles, swinging along with the turns.

Their exit at Passy delivers them to a posher neighborhood. The streets are especially quiet now, on a hot Saturday morning. A short walk brings them to an odd little one-story stucco house, nestled on its tiny lawn in the shade of tall sandstone apartment buildings.

"La Maison Balzac!" Ruth says. "I came here for inspiration when I was taking a class on the nineteenth-century novel." Inside, it's musty but well-preserved: a sitting room, a small bedroom, a study with a big oak desk, stage-set with foolscap and inkpot and quill. And a prominent antique coffee cup. "Balzac was nuts about coffee," she says. "He drank it all day long, and ran all over Paris to get just the right beans."

Mac is peering out the rear window of the study. "Look at this cool little street!" he says.

"Ah, you've discovered the great secret feature of this house. From the front, it seems a modest little bungalow. But it's built on a slope, so there's a floor below this, where the kitchen was. And it opens onto that alley." They head down the narrow stairs. "Balzac was always in debt. When creditors came knocking at the front door, he could slip downstairs, out this door, and down the back street before anyone knew he was gone."

They step into the rue Berton—a narrow passageway lined with high stone walls. There is a single old-style street lamp, and a lantern hanging above the cobblestone alley. "This is one of the few unchanged vestiges of nineteenth-century Paris," Ruth says, as pleased as if it were her private hideout. At the end of a block, they come out on an ugly commercial boulevard, not far from the Seine.

"I *love* it," says Mac. "Whisk-Away Street! I'm building one in Vermont!"

Ruth smiles. She can't see quite where he would contrive such a thing at their tumble-down apartment building in Burlington, or how he'd afford it on the salary of a junior reference librarian, but she likes his enthusiasm. "Are you ready for some *real* coffee?" she asks.

Mac is always ready. They go into Le Balzac, a standard Parisian cafe — plush green velvet banquettes, onyx tabletops, bronzed mirrors on the walls. At this hour between breakfast and lunch, it's practically empty. An older woman sits at the cash register, behind an array of Mars bars and brightly colored cigarette lighters.

Mac asks her, "Ou est le doobla-vay-say?" Ruth cringes; she could have told him where to look. He doesn't have much French, but he has mastered a few key terms. It cracks him up that the word for toilet is "WC," which stands for water closet. "It's a perfectly descriptive term," he says, "but couldn't they think of a French word for it?"

Ruth takes a table, and watches him cross the café. In Vermont, he often wore a baseball cap, but she has told him that will mark him immediately here as American, and why not hold some cards to your chest for a while? She thought he would appreciate the poker metaphor. Not that anyone would doubt his nationality: he strides across the hardwood floor as if he just imposed the Marshall Plan. What is he doing with a woman like her? In the café mirror, she sees a sepia-tinted version of her fine-boned face, looking more like porcelain than usual after a sleepless night. Maybe she should go back to wearing makeup. During her year in Paris, she went for the kohl-eyed look. What has become of the waif she was then?

They drink some real coffee, and she tells Mac the plan. They will walk along the quais, all the way to the Pont Neuf, where they can head north, back towards their room. She especially wants to see le Forum des Halles, the vast central shopping center. They can pick up lunch at a street-side falafel place along the way. It's a long hike, she says, but that's the best way to know a city.

"Point me in the right direction," says Mac, "and I will walk all day."

And so they walk. The river banks are bleaker than Ruth remembered — more auto exhaust, more noise and dirt, fast-food wrappers flying. She wanted Mac, the librarian, to see the *bouquinistes* — those green metal boxes crammed with old books, perched on the stone river walls up and down the Seine. But they are all closed. Is it just too early in the day? Too late in the summer? Or have the book men and women given up the ghost? Beyond the shade of the faded plane trees, the grey-green river rushes on.

Her falafel shop in the rue Saint-André-des-Arts has disappeared. Ruth walks them up and down the street several times, thinking she has just mistaken the exact location. The narrow street is less charming than she remembered.

"I know it was here!" she says, in a block that features window after window of glossy real-estate photos, apartments only a corrupt government official could afford.

"Which side of the street was it?" Mac asks, studying a

poster for télé-sexe.

"I don't know! I thought it would be obvious when I saw the street again! But everything looks different!"

"It's okay, sweetie. You don't have to know. We'll find it — or something else."

Ruth finds herself in the middle of the street, half expecting a garbage truck to run her down. But even the garbage trucks have disappeared. Maybe they only pick up French trash. Let the tourists stew in their mess.

Sweetie? Did he say "sweetie"?

Eventually, they get crêpes from a street-corner griddle on the Place St. Michel. Ruth thinks the ham is dubious — she has read that these vendors get their meat from nearby restaurants when it has passed its sell-by date — but it's food, and nothing would have been as good as the falafel that got away.

They cross the Pont Neuf. Mac keeps intoning "Number Nine, Number Nine," even after Ruth explains that the name has nothing to do with the number; he's just getting a little loopy. It's that time of the afternoon. They peer into the Place Dauphine, where no old men are playing *boules* under the trees. No one is claiming that his ball is closer, drawing a line in the tawny dirt with a linden stick. No jukebox is playing drifty pop music from the open door of a café. The only café is shuttered.

They walk on, across the rue de Rivoli, with its elegant arcades receding to the west, and arrive at a large open space where everything changes. In the background rises the Gothic bulk of St. Eustache — not beautiful, exactly, but imposing its devotional heft. But the foreground is acres of low-lying glass and chrome and steel, cascading into a pit, with escalators trundling people down and out of sight.

"Isn't it ghastly?" says Ruth. "This is what I wrote my dissertation about."

"This?" Mac says. "You had all of Paris to choose from, and you chose this?"

"This used to be Les Halles," she says. "This whole area was a covered market — or rather, an array of covered markets, all of them sheltered by beautiful metal pavilions built in the 1850s. Each one housed its own little world. Not just butchers and cheesemakers and fishmongers, but meat and cheese and fish from a certain province in one pavilion and from another province in the next, with vendors of produce who staked out their places accordingly, and all the accompanying spices and herbs in stalls nearby. It was a vast ecosystem, built up over time; there had been a market here at least as far back as the eleventh century. It was the heart of Paris — or rather, as Zola put it, 'le ventre de Paris,' the belly. Everyone came here, from the most sophisticated restaurateur to the simplest home cook. If you cared about food, you came to Les Halles. And who doesn't care about food in France?"

"Did you get to see it?"

"Oh, no, it was long gone by my time in Paris. They cleared out this whole space back in 1969."

"Why?"

"That's what I wrote about. At the time, the authorities

said they were concerned about traffic and hygiene. They said the trucks snarled up the streets of central Paris, and they told horror stories about rats drawn to rotting food."

"Were they wrong?"

"Of course they were wrong! Does this look better to you?"

"I mean about the traffic and the rats."

"Well, there were a lot of trucks coming and going — but mostly in the wee hours, since the market always opened early. And most of the workers and shoppers walked or took the metro — back when ordinary people could still afford to live in central Paris."

"And the rats?"

"There are *still* rats! Rats gotta live too, you know. But now most of them work in City Hall."

Mac looks again at the pit of glass and chrome. "So what is this Forum thing?"

"It's the real reason they took out Les Halles." Ruth rubbed a thumb against two fingertips. "First, they put an enormous transit hub deep underground. That's a good thing. But then they topped it off with this massive ugly shopping mall. So Instead of the farmers and vendors who used to make small profits and then put them back into other neighborhood shops and cafés and bars, we have T-shirts and sneakers made in Asia at ridiculous prices, alongside fast food sourced from God knows where, and the profits line the pockets of the suits who zip in and out of the city on the hideous highways they built along the banks of the Seine. It's the greatest heist ever perpetrated on a city. They stole its soul."

Mac can only nod. "What's next on the tour, mon capitaine?"

She walks him back down to La Samaritaine, a fine old Art Deco department store overlooking the Pont Neuf. They take the elevator to the ninth floor, where there's a circular rooftop observation deck, with panels that point to all the famous old landmarks — the Eiffel Tower, l'Opéra, la Tour St. Jacques, Sacré-Coeur, la Bastille . . . Ruth points out all the modern desecrations: the towers of La Défense, le Front de Seine, la Place d'Italie, and of course the great abomination, la Tour Maine-Montparnasse, 58 stories of dark glass and steel, right in the heart of the Left Bank. It seems to be flipping the bird to the whole city. "And then, out there in the haze, you can hardly see it today, is the *périphérique* — the peripheral highway that seals off the central city more effectively than any medieval wall ever did. It keeps the lower-class suburbs in their place."

Mac says, "I have to ask: if it's all so awful, why do you love it so much?"

Ruth turns to him. "Because . . . because . . ." She looks at the skyline again. "Because it's Paris," she says. "When you love something, you love it warts and all."

It would be too embarrassing to tell the whole truth — that she feels like she was born here. He knows she was born in New Jersey.

By now it's 2 p.m., and they're hungry again. Mac says, "That crêpe was pretty skinny."

"That's the thing about crêpes."

"Well, I saw that there's a terrace café just one floor down from here."

"Oh, we can't afford that."

"How do you know?"

"It's one of those touristy things; they're always obscenely expensive."

Mac pulls a wad of francs from his pocket. "But look at all this pretty cash," he says. "It's like play money! I especially like the hundreds, because they're bigger." He squints at a bill. "Hey, Delacroix was a good-lookin' dude."

"Put that away!" Ruth says. "Some pickpocket is sizing you up as we speak."

Mac looks around the deck, which contains two German tourists in hiking shorts and boots. "Let's eat here," he says.

"But—"

He holds the hundred-franc note with two fingers out over the railing. "We eat here, or Eugene goes flying," he says.

"Mac—"

He flourishes the note in the warm breeze. "Somebody's going to be happy down below."

She acquiesces, but she only orders a salad. And a double espresso—she's starting to get woozy with jetlag. Mac gets steak frites, and a glass of red wine, and a café Américain, which means a full-size cup, with cream, instead of those stingy little demitasses. And then, to top it off, he orders two glasses of Calvados.

"Mac!"

The waiter looks at them inquiringly. "Monsieur dame?" Do they want the Calvados or not?

"Deux," says Mac, holding up a peace sign. The *garçon* nods and leaves.

Ruth sighs. "Actually," she says, "the French count starting with the thumb, so they signal two like this," and she counts one-two, thumb-pointer.

"Tray bien," says Mac, in his finest Vermont French. "Let's enjoy our Calvados."

Ruth has to admit that it's exquisite.

"Et maintenant?" Mac sings. "What now, my love?" He may not know much French, but he knows his dumb old pop songs.

"I thought it might be good if we each had a little alone time," she says.

He looks crestfallen. "Did I say something wrong? I thought you liked the Calvados!"

"I did! And no, you didn't say anything wrong. But don't you think it would be good if we both had a little decompression time? I thought we should probably do this every day."

"I thought this was our big holiday together," he says.

"Yes, but—"

"You want to sneak back to the room and take a nap!"

"I do not!" she exclaims—though now that he mentions it, a nap sounds heavenly.

"So what will you do?"

"I'm dying for some greenery. There's supposed to be

a new 'eco-quarter' not too far northeast of here, along the Canal Saint-Martin. I've got to see what they're up to. And you? What would you like to do?"

"I don't know. This ain't my town."

"Well, I can make some suggestions. Can you get out the map?" In a pocket of his cargo pants, Mac is carrying a big Michelin map, folded many times.

"Nope," he says.

"What?"

"I don't need no stinkin' map."

"But where will you go?"

"That's the great adventure."

She is dumbstruck. He goes on.

"You know what my father used to say? 'Life is like driving a car at night. You can only see as far as your headlights, but you can make the whole trip that way.' I'm going to wander. We can meet back at the room."

He is eager to get started; she needs to use the WC. When she gets back to the table, he has cleared out, leaving a stack of play money on the table. When are they supposed to meet? Oh well, she thinks, probably something like five o'clock. It's three o'clock now. She lifts a fifty-franc note from the table. She needs to explain the concept of *service compris*.

She sets out walking, north and east from the river. But after the clear landmark of the Beaubourg, with its great sloping plaza full of buskers and merrymakers—she lingers for a while by a woman who is pounding at an electric keyboard, wearing a headset of lights that blink crazily in time to her playing—she gets a bit turned around in the warren of streets beyond. Tabac at the corner, pharmacy, café, tiny grocery, couscous restaurant—block after block seem the same. Back in her Paris year, she was never in this neighborhood. Mac has kept the map stubbornly in his pocket. Well, she will find a landmark soon enough, if only a metro stop, with its handy "Vous Êtes Ici" display.

At a crossing, she comes upon a little park—half a city block of trees and well-groomed sandy paths leading to an open space with playground equipment. She loves these little pocket parks, which are so vital to their neighborhoods. Pushing through the green metal gate, she steps in.

It was in just such a park that she lived through her great crisis, nine years before. That whole year had been crisis after crisis, starting with the cleavage from her parents, who had not wanted her to go. Her father told her how impractical it was to spend a year in France just when she needed to push ahead her pre-med studies, consolidating her resumé for the arduous med school applications of the year to come. She assured him that she had it under control, that she could complete all the required courses in her senior year, and med schools really liked to see evidence of a well-rounded, adventurous candidate. Her mother feared for her safety in the big city: "I hear it's full of Arabs now, and you know they have different ideas about women." Ruth promised she would be careful. She would write a letter every week. Her mother persuaded her father that it would be OK.

Three weeks into the new school year, she met a man—a French man named Yvon. She made eye contact in the metro, as she had been warned not to do. He got off at her stop, caught up to her on the sidewalk, invited her for coffee. That was the beginning of a hectic love affair— her "nouvelle vague romance," as she described it to her American roommate, Jenny, a nice girl from Ohio. Ruth saw it all in black and white—stolen kisses, love on the run. He was married, of course. He lived in Dijon, but kept an apartment in Paris for business purposes. As far as she could tell, she was his business. He took her to cafés and restaurants she could never have afforded, and they saw all the old movies they could, in the few little repertory cinemas that remained. Their romance blossomed in the dark.

She had had boyfriends in high school and college, but never anything to rival this. She was not a pretty girl in any classic way: her face was too round, her hair too crinkly, her hips too broad, no matter how she dieted. She thought this was why her father pushed her towards medicine; a girl who looked like her would need a career. Yvon seemed to sense all this. He urged her to take her hair out of its barrettes and let crinkliness be a virtue; he bought her dangly silver earrings that elongated her face, and silky camisoles that made her forget her hips. He himself was not handsome: he was tall and ungainly, with dark five o'clock shadow and uneven teeth. But he was hers. He told her she was like Jeanne Moreau in a greasepaint mustache and a checkered cap, running across a bridge; she was transgressive, she was *farouche*. How could she resist?

She kept up cordial relations with her French family and Jenny; she checked in to do laundry and chat. But she stopped hanging out with the other kids from their program; she was always out with Yvon, or else holed up in his little pied-à-terre near the Gare de Lyon, where they spent whole weekends drinking coffee, listening to Paul Desmond on an old turntable, and making love. She called herself Marie-Ange now. She had never cared for the name Ruth, and the French pronunciation made it sound like a German legume. Sometimes, walking from the metro to Yvon's place, she narrated her own life aloud in a hushed voice-over, in the third person. "Marie-Ange had never wanted to be married or have children. She wanted to plumb the depths of love."

She stopped writing home. The sunny letters about zose cra-zee French had been full of lies and half-truths, anyway. At Christmas, she sent a card to explain that she couldn't afford to fly home, but she'd be thinking of them. She barely kept up with her classes — but as everyone knows, study abroad never puts much emphasis on the first word. She did enough. When Yvon was out of town, she focused like a laser on Les Halles. That project, she was sure, would explain what was wrong with Paris, and how it could be set right again.

And then, in a little park on a gorgeous April afternoon,

everything came crashing down. She sat on a bench with Yvon and told him that her year was ending, and she didn't want to leave. He smiled. He took her chin in hand and told her he adored her. And then—of course—he said that all good things must end. She was on a student visa, *non*? His business in Paris was ending, too, and he was giving up the apartment. His wife and children needed him. And she—Ruth—needed to get back to her "real life" in the U.S. He even sang a little bit of a song from her favorite movie, in his swift, clipped baritone:

Chacun pour soi est reparti

Dans le tourbillon de la vie . . .

"Each of them left alone, into the whirlwind of life." It was too cruel. Paris *was* her real life! That other life, college and her parents' suburban home, had been nothing but sleepwalking for twenty years. Was it true, what he said about his business in Paris ending? Had her visa been part of his calculation all along? She couldn't know. But she knew it was over. They made love one last time in that little apartment that had been the heart's blood of her year—of her life, so far. She cried the whole time. They never saw each other again.

Returning to the States, she got another surprise. She had expected that her parents would be furious about her failures of communication, that her father would be on her case about medical school even more intensely now. Instead, they hardly seemed to notice that she was back. They themselves were breaking up, in a storm of rancor. Her father had moved to an apartment in the city; her mother was soaking in white wine with commiserating friends. For the summer before her senior year, she stayed with her mother in the old New Jersey house. But it was not home; it was a staging ground for that final year, which would launch her God knew where. The one thing she had, as she contemplated her prospects, was the passion awakened by Les Halles. Back on campus, she signed up for a whole raft of courses on environmental studies. A year later, she was in Vermont, working for scraps at a nonprofit focused on the environment. But she could live on scraps — it was part of the ethic. She kept her head down. She did good work. She had a few desultory hookups, but always held back from anything like commitment. In a couple of years, she was given a full scholarship to the fledgling Environmental Studies program at the university. And then one day, pursuing some research on the right-of-way for an extension of the Burlington bike path, she met this lanky rusty-haired librarian who was eager to help.

On the bench in her little park, she is starting to nod off. Across the street, there is a small café. A cappuccino would be the right thing to perk her up for the walk back to their room. It's delicious — but really too hot for such a sultry afternoon. She remembers what the workers at Les Halles would have for refreshment early in the day — *un petit vin blanc sec*. A nice little dry white wine. It isn't in her budget for the day — but she has that fifty-franc note she hadn't counted on. She sits in a chair with wooden slats on the tiny sidewalk terrace of the café, in the shade of a green awning, and watches some kids playing in the park.

When she gets up, a little buzzed, she wanders aimlessly for a while, but eventually crosses a street she knows, and angles back toward their room. By the time she gets there, it is well after six. And there is no sign of Mac.

Well, he didn't name a specific hour. She was the one who said they should have some time apart. At the sink, she soaks a washtowel in cold water, then lays it across her face. She turns on the little transistor radio she brought: news she doesn't want to know. Then she lies down, just to stretch out her legs.

He is standing in front of a stegosaurus. Or rather, the skeleton of a stegosaurus, beautifully reconstructed, with only a few spots where missing bones have been supplanted by bone-colored plaster. He has wandered by the Seine, lingered at the Holocaust memorial at the back of the Ile de la Cité, sat in the shade of the oldest tree in Paris, browsed at Shakespeare and Company, then strolled for a while in the Jardin des Plantes, before discovering that those gorgeous gardens are really just a front for this magnificent museum full of rocks and stones and bones. Mac is a sucker for natural history. If he could have pursued any field in the world, it would have been paleontology. But after growing up on a farm outside of Bristol, Vermont, he feared that dinosaur bones would be a stretch for a career. He was already the first in his family to go beyond high school; better not to press his luck. He had always liked libraries, and every little town had one. He went off to Syracuse for two years, and came home to a job at the biggest library in Vermont, up at the university.

Fortunately, his older brother wanted to stay and work the farm, so Mac didn't feel guilty about abandoning it. He *was* abandoning it — but he let the extended family believe that he was just conceding the right of primogeniture to Tom. Then both of their parents died, in quick succession, and Mac got even more committed to library work. It was good to know things; it gave you a purchase on the world, which was clearly slippery enough.

All of this was fine with Tom, as long as Mac came home for Christmas and the occasional Sunday dinner. When it came to dating Ruth, though, Tom was not so sure. He had voiced the doubts in a conversation earlier that summer, out on the old front porch.

"Are you sure about this woman, bro?"

"Why do you ask?"

"Well, she's . . . kinda Jewish, isn't she?"

"You did *not* just say that."

"You know what I mean. She can worship any day of the week for all I care, but she's such a city chick, and you're still a country boy, even if you did run off to Syracuse for a while."

Mac smiled at the idea of Syracuse as the metropolis. "Yes," he said, "she is of the Hebrew faith. And yes, she's a little more polished than your typical woodchuck girl; she will not be on the line-dancing float in the Fourth of July parade." This was a direct shot at Tom's Callie, who had been head of the line for three years running. "But perhaps I am not quite as rough-hewn as you seem to assume."

"I just hate to see you living in that rat-hole apartment in Burlington, when you could rent a whole farmhouse down here for the same amount. Or a house in town, for that matter. You know they're opening an organic market on East Street."

"And drive an hour each way to our jobs in Burlington? That would hardly be environmentally sensitive."

"See, that's what I mean. All this sensitivity can't be good for you. What happened to the kid so tough that no one dared to call him Eustace?"

"You'll find out soon enough, if you keep dissing Ruth."

He did not tell his brother the deeper truth—that he had come to see Ruth as his fate, for good or ill. That he loved the complexity of her—the spiky idealist who brooded over global warming before most people knew what it was. That he relished the challenge presented by her occasional spells of chilliness. In the early months of their acquaintance, he hadn't been able to tell if she was scared or just uninterested. She probably had her own versions of the questions Tom had raised so inelegantly. Wasn't he . . . . kinda backwoods? Did he really care about those stupid sports teams? Would he understand her passionate activism?

Well, here he is in Paris. Standing in front of a stegosaurus, which is pretty freakin' cool. He feels that he is on the verge of something big. He has found the Red Sox score in the *International Herald Tribune.* They won. Life is good.

Ruth snorts out of her sleep when she hears someone at the door. The room has gone dark. How long was she asleep? She rises from bed to stand by the window, as if she has been there all the while. Dear God, she thinks, let it be Mac.

He flips the wall switch.

"Hey, what are you doing in the dark?"

"Just appreciating *le crépuscule du soir*," she says.

He nods. He is carrying several bulging plastic bags. He sets them on the bare table in the middle of the room.

"Sorry I'm late," he says. "Am I late? Well, sorry if you were waiting." He points to the bags as if they're treasures from the deep. "I brought Chinese!" He starts pulling out white cartons. "I had no idea how to order, so I just pointed at the menu." The cartons keep coming, piling up on the table like a medieval fortress of white cardboard boxes. "Maybe I overdid it?" From another bag he draws a bottle of wine, and also—"ta-dah!"—a squat little bottle of Calvados. "You won't believe how cheap it was! I hope it's not rotgut." And then from another sack comes a baker's box full of pastries. "Full disclosure: if the girl at the patisserie hadn't been so cute, I might not have bought quite so many. What's *crépuscule*?"

He notices that she is looking at him aghast, her shoulders sagging. "Not as cute as *you*, of course."

She says, "Mac. How are we going to eat all that? It's way too much. We don't have a refrigerator for leftovers! It's wasteful. And you know how I feel about plastic bags."

He stares. "It was the only kind they had! I asked for *un bag de papier*, I swear! Of course, maybe they didn't understand my French."

"Great," she says. "You asked them for a paper ring." She touches her empty ring finger.

"Oh. Oh well. I thought they looked at me funny. I promise to use these bags all week for all the stuff we buy from now on, and to take them back to Vermont, and — and — to line planters with them. Or something. OK? Can we eat while it's hot? I'm famished."

She smiles. What can she do? "Did you get a corkscrew?"

He reaches into one of his deep pockets. "Voilà," he says, and tweaks his invisible mustache.

"*Crépuscule*," she says, "means twilight. But you can say it about either dusk or dawn, which is *le crépuscule du matin*. That's where we get our word 'crepuscular.'"

"I like it," he says. "Score one for the Frogs."

Of course she wakes in the middle of the night. Her internal clock is in ruins. How many coffees has she had? How much wine and Calvados? General Tso's chicken sits on her stomach like a tumor to be excised. She has to get down the hall to the WC. She tries to roll off her single bed with a minimum of noise, and then she realizes, focusing on the other bed in the ambered city dark, that it is empty.

"Mac?"

There is no reply. It's a small room. She is the only person in it.

She fumbles her way down the dark hall to the toilet: first things first. On the way back, she tells herself, "Marie-Ange was so jetlagged that she was seeing things. Or not seeing things, when in fact things were there." But things are not there. Still no Mac. Now there is no chance that she will get back to sleep. She stands by the window and looks out over the rooftops. In the eastern distance, a pale blue glow hovers just above the chimneypots.

This is crazy. What are they doing? It's only ten days until classes began again, and she has so much work to do. She has no business dawdling with this unpredictable man in Paris, as if she still belonged here. Her father was right: she wasn't cut out for relationships. Poor goofy Mac has no idea what he's getting into. She should call the whole thing off. It will be painful, but they both will be better off in the long run. Maybe he realized this in the night. Maybe that's why the lovemaking was so intense: it was farewell sex, we're done sex. Maybe Mac is out wandering the boulevards, taking down télé-sex numbers, planning his solo return to Vermont. Maybe he is hooking up with that pastry-shop girl.

The sky has paled over before she hears the door opening slowly behind her.

"Hey, you're up!" he says.

"Where have you been?"

"I couldn't sleep. It's incredible out there. You'd never believe that so much was going on before dawn. I walked up this *rue*, whatever it's called—"

"La rue du Faubourg Poissonière."

"Yeah, that. Until I came to a metro stop, up there with the elevated track?"

"Barbès-Rochechouart."

"Couldn't they find something a little harder to pronounce? And underneath the tracks, there was this whole little city. All these African dudes, some of them wearing dashikis, camped out with sleeping bags and cardboard boxes."

"Did you talk to them?" Ruth is still a little bit afraid among the dark-skinned Parisians on the edges of the city. She isn't proud of it. She blames her mother's warnings from years ago.

He brandishes an empty plastic bag. "I gave them the leftovers! I had thought I would just sit in a park and feed the pigeons, you know, but then I saw these guys, and I thought what the heck. And man, those guys loved me. It was Chinese breakfast at Whatchacallit."

"You're amazing," she says.

"On my good days." He nods at the sky. "Look at that light rising. It's downright corpuscular out there. You wanna step out for coffee?"

It isn't easy to find coffee that early, but of course there is a Starbucks on the grands boulevards. This violates every principle of Ruth's plan for the week, and also her vision of the universe—but the flat white venti speaks to her in tongues.

They sit by a window and watch the light rise. Early workers bustle by, intent on inner worlds. This is the beauty of a city: so many lives in play, so much energy afoot. Each time she sees someone with earbuds, she wants to pull them out and shout, "Réveillez-vous! Wake up! Your life is out here!"

Mac clears his throat. "I brung you somefing." When things veer serious, he gets demotic.

From his breast pocket he pulls a little hunk of—what? Paper? It seems to be newsprint, compacted and twisted so it will hold a circular shape. He takes her left hand from the table, and holds it before him. He poises the bit of paper in front of it.

"With this ring," he says—

She pulls her hand back. He takes it again.

" —I thee wed." And he pushes the ring on her bare ring finger. The paper tears a little, but it holds.

She pulls her hand back again. "Mac, you can't joke about this."

"Who's joking?"

She remains silent. He goes on.

"I plight my troth."

"Mac." It's a Starbucks on the Boulevard Montmartre. It's too ridiculous.

"I've only got so much troth," he says. "Take it or leave it."

They got married later that week, in the *mairie* of the tenth arrondissement. Mac got one of the African guys to serve as their witness. It wasn't clear if the man knew what he had agreed to do, but he showed up in a fine dashiki. Ruth wore her knee-high boots, instead of the usual sneakers. Mac plucked a primrose from a windowbox and tucked it in the shaggy hair above his ear. Afterward, they ate Chinese takeaway on a bench in the Square Montholon. The heat and humidity had lifted. High above them, thin white clouds were etched on a pale lacquer sky.

A young woman sits on a bench in a little park in Paris, weeping. Just minutes ago, her tall companion walked away, letting the gate swing shut with a clang. Her life is over. She cannot imagine how to carry on from here. People walking past look away; it's too raw and private for everyday eyes. She doesn't notice. She is inconsolable.

A man stands in front of a stegosaurus, overcome with awe. To think that no human being ever saw such a beast, and yet we are able to imagine it, to string together the bones and understand how it must have lived. What it ate and drank, how it fended off enemies, how long it strode the earth. It's all too much. Or almost too much. He can't wait to tell his sweetheart about it.

Carrying Capacity

The Earth and all its residents are doomed. Polar bears are clinging to ever-shrinking ice floes. Coral reefs are in steep decline; they may be gone entirely in thirty years. Even insects, which once seemed to be the sure survivors of us all, are in retreat. A 2017 study from a nature preserve in Germany documented that over the past three decades the number of flying insects had diminished by more than seventy-five per cent.

So says Kevin, and he should know — he's the instructor of Environmental Studies 101 at the community college. Harper, in the second row, gives him her full attention as he stands before the class, pointing to a screen dense with graphs and numbers. His short black hair sets off a pale complexion, and a gold earring glints above his black turtleneck. On a wintry day in Winooski, his boot-cut jeans show off a pair of gleaming black calf-high boots.

Harper has heard most of this before. She grew up at talks like this, thanks to her mother, who teaches Environmental Studies at the university. But she hasn't heard about the baiji, a freshwater dolphin, also known as the Goddess of the Yangtze. Kevin says the baiji is now functionally extinct: if any still exist, the number is too small for the species to survive. The last verified sighting was in 2011, seven years ago. But just last year a Chinese fisherman reported that he saw one leaping in the distance. Harper wants to head for the Yangtze right away, to see the last baiji before it's too late.

Instead, after class she walks out to the city bus that will take her up to the medical center, where her mother is undergoing treatment. Ruth receives a two-hour chemo infusion once a week, to keep her cancer in check. She has tried to shoo Harper away, saying surely she has better things to do. She could be reading for that class she's auditing; better yet, she could be working on her G.E.D. But Harper is not an academic rocket like her mother was; she is a high school dropout, with a boatload of credits to go. And she is in no hurry. She doesn't know what she would do after high school, anyway. Why rush the unknown?

When she arrives at the chemo bay, her mother is already asleep, zonked on Benadryl. Each patient sits in a big recliner, flanked by an IV machine that titrates the medicine. There are four bays, each consisting of four chairs arranged in a square, so the patients face each other as if awaiting the call for allemande left. Each bay has its own nurse sitting at a central table, monitoring the infusions. Today Ruth is in a chair by the window that looks out across a little courtyard garden—a blessing on a dim December morning. In her sleep, with her glasses off, her round face looks blurred; her frizzy dark hair, thinned by the treatments, corkscrews in unplanned directions. Harper is quietly greeted by the nurse, who has seen her here before. Settling into a straight-back chair by the window, she takes out her ES notes.

Kevin says that humans are the problem. While other species dwindle, humans continue to multiply. Three billion, seven billion, ten billion: we seem to know no limits. And why should we accept limits, with our big brains, opposable thumbs, and myths about being favored by the gods? We disrupt and appropriate the habitats of other creatures. We feed our miserable livestock on land that used to be forest, lungs for the planet. We pump CO_2 into the sky, because our cars are so convenient. As global temperatures rise and the polar ice caps shrink, there's more open water, which absorbs more sunlight, which causes more ice to melt, which leaves more open water, which absorbs more sunlight, which causes more ice to melt, which . . .

It's a broken planet. But Harper has always known this. Although her parents did not take her to temple as a child — her father, a lapsed Presbyterian, would not have been involved, in any case — her mother made sure she knew about *tikkun olam*, repairing the world. According to the Kabbalah, the whole creation was shattered at its inception, scattered into millions of shards. Our task, her mother said, is to retrieve the fragments and piece them together again. This can't be done quickly; it can't be done in a lifetime, or a millennium. But it's still our task.

At the chair that faces Ruth's, something isn't right. The patient, a heavy-set man with tufts of white hair above his ears, has started gasping. His face is drained of color. When the nurse asks what's wrong, he can't seem to speak. His companion, a small woman in a red Christmas sweater, stands up from her chair and exclaims, "Oh my God! Oh my God!" The nurse shuts down the man's infusion and signals for help from the charge nurse, who, working in a glass-enclosed office at the center of the four chemo bays, has already seen that something is amiss. She is on a cell phone, calling for help. Within minutes, the small space around the man's chair is filled by nurses and EMTs, someone with oxygen, someone with a gurney. The man's companion looks on from the central office, her face ashen. The charge nurse, a sturdy young woman with dark unruly hair and black-framed glasses, tells the bay nurse to push saline through the IV. There's a long silence. Everyone in the bay focuses on the patient, who is scrabbling for breath.

Then he coughs, sputters, and croaks, "What's happening to me?"

"You're going to be OK," the charge nurse says. "It was probably a reaction to the chemo. Sometimes the body doesn't want to deal with it."

The attending oncologist arrives, lab coat swishing over a fashionable skirt, and confirms the charge nurse's analysis. "More saline," she says. "We'll find a different treatment."

Harper feels her body relax. In front of her, two blue-

suited EMTs start chatting about their plans for the weekend. She turns to check on her mother. Ruth has slept
through the whole thing.

Harper packs up her notes; she has things to do before
her evening shift at Pho Hong. She will get no credit for
sitting by her mother's side, but Ruth would approve of
her next errand. She nods goodbye to the bay nurse, who
will be left to wrestle with Ruth over driving home too
soon after the infusion. Harper knows who will win that
argument.

She catches the shuttle bus down the hill into central
Burlington, and gets out by Stone Soup, where she gets
a scone and coffee. Sitting at the back counter, she can
look into the open kitchen. She likes watching the young
women — it always seems to be young women — rolling
out cylinders of dough, hoisting trays into the big silver
oven, removing the fragrant loaves. Over a second mug
of coffee, she imagines the whole world held together by
bread dough, yeasty in its rising. Then she pulls a clipboard and pen from her backpack and walks on down
the block. She's got a coffee buzz on now; she's ready for
the street.

Anyone who knew Harper two years ago would be
amazed. At sixteen, she shaved off her long blond hair,
ran off with a boyfriend, and lived with him in a farmhouse where some older friends let them crash until
they got themselves together. The boyfriend's idea of
getting himself together was sleeping with one of the
other women, who liked his nonchalance. Harper, to her

surprise, discovered that she didn't. She had thought it was cool not to be jealous; after all, it was just sex. But she *was* jealous. It *wasn't* just sex. It was how you treated people.

Lying about her age—she had always been tall, and could pass for eighteen—she got a job washing dishes at Pho Hong, and moved back in with her mother, who promised not to give her grief about high school. Since her father had cleared out several years before, it seemed a good arrangement: in the little house on Louise Street, where Harper grew up, the two abandoned females could keep each other company. In fact, they seldom see each other. By the time Harper gets the bus home from the restaurant, her mother, so easily tired now, is already in bed. When Harper gets up in the morning, Ruth is off to work on campus.

With her wide hazel eyes and her crooked nose, broken at birth, Harper has a disarming look that's good for collecting signatures. Of course, some people turn away as soon as they see the clipboard. But in a college town like Burlington, someone will always stop and engage with her, curious about her cause. Why is this tall young woman in the silver down coat and the navy watch cap out on the street in the cold, asking for a minute of their time?

"It's all about the trees," she explains to a middle-aged man in similar winter gear. "Do you live in Burlington?" The man says yes. "Then you know City Hall Park, right?" She points in its direction, just a block from the bricked-over main shopping street where they stand. He nods; any Burlingtonian knows the little park in the center of town.

"So you know it's the only green space downtown. It's been a park since, like, 1800, and some of the trees date back that far, too. It's an oasis, the kind of quiet space every city needs." The man nods; he's ready for her spiel. "But now City Council has decided that the park needs renovation, and their plan calls for chopping down a third of the trees! They say it's necessary for the 'improvements' they have in mind — wider sidewalks, more concrete, better foot traffic flow. Their plan calls for kiosks that will sell coffee and sandwiches; maybe that's why they want better traffic flow, to milk some money from the park. But there are already eleventy-seven places to get coffee within two blocks! Do we really need to cut down those great old trees just to sell sandwiches?" She's rolling now; the man is clearly with her. "And the thing is, nobody ever voted for this! City Council just decided those old trees need to go! Some of us don't want to lose them. So we're collecting signatures on this petition to put the renovation on the ballot. Let the people have a say!"

The man signs and says good luck, he'll look for it when he votes.

"Bravo!" a familiar voice exclaims. It's Kevin, earring glinting under a maroon woolen cap. "You had that guy eating out of your hand."

She feels a flush of pleasure on the back of her neck. "Well, how could you be against the trees?"

"The city arborist says those trees are already dying, and their root systems are choking out the grass."

"But—"

"And the grass is already in terrible shape, because the soil is so compacted by all the foot traffic going off the sidewalks, especially during Farmers Market."

"Yes, but—"

"They say the slight increase in concrete will actually improve plant life, because it will give people clear and adequate paths, allowing the grass to revive. Plus," he adds before she can interject, "the current sidewalk is so steep that it's out of compliance with the Americans with Disabilities Act. The new design is wheelchair-accessible. Hard to argue with that."

"We just want to let the people vote," she says.

"But they already voted—to elect City Councilors who would study these things and make informed decisions. When you let the people decide, you get results like Brexit."

She drops her hands to her hips. "Whose side are you on?"

"I'm on the side of reasoned debate." He looks up at the clock above the street. "I gotta jet. See you in class."

And he's off. She is deflated, and cold. But she got another signature. And at least Kevin knows who she is.

The next day, Saturday, as she's walking to work in the Old North End, she stops dead at the corner of Archibald Street. There are hundreds of old green trucks in Vermont, but even before she gets close enough to check the license plate, she knows that this one, parked near the old synagogue, belongs to her father. Five years ago, she looked for it in the driveway every morning. After three months, she decided that if he ever did come back, she would not speak to him. Even as she hated him, she has missed him every day.

She knows it's silly to imagine that Sloppy Joe could be alive. He was already half-gone when her father left, taking the old dog with him. But still she can't help peering into the cab, looking for a blanket covered with dog hair. All she sees is her own reflection.

*

It began with a small resolution, soon after he started crashing in Stan's office on North Winooski Avenue. Every time he stepped outside, he would pick up at least one piece of litter and drop it in the nearest bin. It seemed like the least he could do in exchange for a place to sleep. As the days went by, he found himself picking up more and more trash, stuffing the pockets of his old brown corduroy coat. One day, he took a Hefty bag from the galley kitchen, and within a couple of hours it was full. He duct-taped a tenpenny nail to a sturdy towel rod, enabling him to spear bits of paper without bending down. Now he walks for two or three hours a day, from Battery Park to the edge of the Intervale, up to Mount St. Joseph Cemetery, then down through the student enclave near downtown before heading back up North Winooski to reward himself with a muffin at a bakery called Knead. He doesn't venture into the city center; let someone else pick up after the tourists.

Stan's office space is surprisingly comfortable. There's a pull-out sofa-bed that Mac pushes back into place every morning; there's the little kitchen, where he microwaves things he picks up from the deli down the street; there's a decent bathroom in the hall, complete with the wonder of a shower. Mac has slept in dodgier places in the past five years. He keeps the thermostat low, not wanting to run up the gas bill. He just needs to be out of the way before eight thirty, when Stan, his old high school friend, starts his day as the coordinator of a non-profit that provides home care for people with special needs. When Mac first appeared at the door three weeks ago, he joked about his own special needs. Stan, who had heard this line before, said, "You just need a haircut."

Stan is a big guy in his late forties, with short dark hair and a well-trimmed beard. He looks like he could crush you if he wanted to—but he would never want to. Like Mac, he has had his adventures with women and drink and knuckleheaded behavior. Unlike Mac, he seems to have settled for good. Mac knew better than to trouble him at home: Stan's wife, another old classmate, would not be thrilled to see him. But when he appeared at the office, Stan tossed him a set of keys and said, "For a while."

In these five years, Mac has been a short-order cook, a handyman, a gardener, and a bouncer. He has sold Christmas trees. He has driven an Uber. Now, thanks to

Stan's hospitality, he picks up trash, unpaid. All his earthly goods — a few changes of clothing, a shaving kit, a well-furnished toolbox — fit easily in the truck. The real challenge is finding a parking spot that won't lead to getting towed.

It's strange to be back in Burlington. At thirty, he thought he would never leave. At forty-three, he thought he would never come back. Now, at forty-eight, he doesn't know what he thinks. Stan, who stays in touch with the old Addison County crowd, reports that Mac's brother Tom is still soldiering on down there. His two sons are grown and gone; he and his wife play bridge in Middlebury. At their father's funeral fifteen years ago, Tom told Mac he would always be welcome to come help on the farm; there was plenty of room in the old house. Mac thanked him and thought, *No way.* He had watched his father deflate in that work, year after year, as the big corporate farms grew up around them. That was why Mac went to graduate school. As Ernest Shackleton used to say, better a live donkey than a dead lion.

He is determined not to bother Ruth. He stays away from their old South End neighborhood; he stays away from the university, where she works, and from downtown, where she shops. He knows he doesn't deserve her attention now. But he feels an invisible filament that connects him to his daughter. And he doesn't know, yet, what to do about it.

Once, in his previous incarnation as a reference librarian, he helped a student who was doing a project on Agatha Christie. The word *mystery*, he learned, comes from *muo,* which is also the source of the word *mute.* Literally, it means "to shut the mouth." It is that which leaves us speechless.

Most nights, Harper is good at waiting tables. She is attentive and friendly; she likes helping people have a good time. But on this evening, she is off her game. It starts with a pitcher of water that slides off a platter, crashing to the cement floor in a thousand pieces. Then there is a wailing child who cannot be satisfied, despite her deployment of crayons and after-dinner mints. In the kitchen, she admits to Jimmy, the head cook, "I think I'm going to kill that kid." It doesn't help when a crew of college students—a table for eight made of two tables that she helped them push together—stiffs her on the tip. After she misplaces an order, delaying service for a four-top of young professionals, Jimmy says, "Why don't you take the rest of the night off?"

"Really?"

"Yeah." A tall black guy in an orange baseball cap, Jimmy says he's "on hiatus" from the university. If so, he must have been on hiatus for fifteen years. He looks at the dining room, now slowing down. "Josie's got it covered. Right, Jose?"

Josie, a senior at St. Michael's and a Pho Hong veteran, says, "Sure. More tips for me."

Harper doesn't want to let them down, but if the rest of her shift brings further disarray, she won't be helping the cause. She hangs her apron on a hook by the kitchen door and pulls on the big down coat. She says to Josie, "Let me know if you need me to cover a shift sometime." And she's out the door.

When she crosses Archibald, the truck is still there. Usually, on a cold night like this, she would catch the bus that takes her within a few blocks of her mother's house in the South End. But tonight she doesn't want to linger at the bus stop. It's a thirty-minute walk. She tugs the watch cap more firmly over her ears. By the time she gets home, her mother will be asleep.

In fact, when she steps into her mother's kitchen, she finds that Ruth is very much awake, sitting at the table with her laptop in the yellow glow of the hanging lamp.

"Harper! I'm glad you're home."

"What are you doing up, Mom?" Her mother doesn't look good. She's often tired now, but tonight she is positively haggard.

"Someone has defaced the synagogue."

"What?"

"Look." Her mother points at the laptop.

On the screen, there's a grainy photograph of the old red-brick building with its short double staircase leading to the front entrance from either side. Across one of the two white doors, in raw black paint, someone has scrawled a swastika.

"Oh!" is all she can say at first. Then: "Who?"

Ruth shakes her head. "It just appeared this morning."

Harper sits down at the table, still muffled in the big down coat. "Why?"

Her mother doesn't even try to address that one.

Early on Sunday afternoon, Ruth drives them both up to Archibald Street. Harper prays that the truck will not be parked where it was yesterday.

It's not. Out in front of the synagogue, a little crowd has gathered. The stairs have been blocked off with yellow tape. The streaks of black paint look even more lurid in person.

One of the people on the sidewalk greets Ruth. It's Doris Lashman, a member of the congregation who also works at the university. Her voice is hushed. "Isn't it horrifying?"

Ruth nods wearily.

Doris says, "I'm going to get some turpentine."

"No!" Ruth is suddenly animated. "This is a hate crime! The police need to investigate! The evidence must stand. Let it be a marker of their shame."

Harper looks on in silence. What is there to say? The thing is, she thinks she knows who did it.

Back on Louise Street, Ruth has papers to grade; Harper says she wants to take a walk. In five minutes, she's at the apartment building down on Pine.

She passes by here often—it's where the bus stop is—but she hasn't been inside for years. It's a boxy two-story complex that extends for most of a city block, hugging the sidewalk and the busy thoroughfare of Pine Street. This is where her old boyfriend Josh grew up. She doesn't

know where he lives now, but on a December Sunday afternoon, he's just where she thought he'd be: in the darkened living room, watching the Patriots with his old man.

He looks surprised to see her at the door. Two years
ago, when he went to work for the construction company
where his father is a foreman, he got his long dark hair
cut short; it is still closely cropped, giving him a military
air. Wearing a baggy black sweatshirt, he's as skinny and
pale as ever, and he still has those high cheekbones. His
dark eyes fix on hers.

"Don't people phone or text these days?"

He doesn't mumble the way he used to do. She misses it.

"I don't know what people do. Do you want to take a
walk?"

He looks at his father, engrossed in the TV. His mother
disappeared long ago. Harper can see him calculate
whether he can get back for the end of the game. He puts
on the same dark thrift-store coat he wore when they
were together.

As if on automatic pilot, they walk to the park at the
edge of her mother's neighborhood, where they used to
hang out, smoking and getting high. Soon they're sitting
on the jungle gym, just as they used to do.

"What's up?" he asks. His breath hangs before him in
the frosty air. There's the staticky smell of a snowstorm
brewing.

"This isn't good, Josh."

"What isn't?"

"The swastika at the synagogue."

"I heard about that."

"It isn't cool."

"Why are you telling me?"

"You don't have to play innocent."

"I don't know what you're talking about. You don't think I did it?"

"No. I don't think you're that stupid. But I think Breiner and Ronan are."

He doesn't speak. Breiner and Ronan are his old friends, and Harper's right: they're stupid. They've done this kind of thing before. She doesn't think they're anti-Semitic, exactly. They might have thought a swastika on a synagogue was funny; they might have done it on a dare. They might have fallen in with the wrong websites.

"Tell them it's serious," she says. "Tell them it's not just tagging. It's considered a hate crime, and the cops could take it straight to the FBI."

Her mother would be furious with her. Her father would understand.

Josh looks across the playground, empty on an icy afternoon. The short December daylight is drawing down. "Want to crack some ice?" he says.

It's something they used to do: walk all the sidewalks of the neighborhood on a cold day, looking for iced-over puddles. When they found one, they took turns stomping on it with their boots. Some of the puddles exploded in icy splashes; others, deeper and denser, held their weight at first, shivering into branching cracks. Those were the good ones.

"Sure," she says, and they stomp off together.

When Mac comes into the office that afternoon, after dropping his Hefty bag in the dumpster behind the building, he finds Stan sitting on the sofa in the gathering dusk, still wearing his big pea coat.

"Mr. Philips! What brings you in on a Sunday?"

"I think you should talk to your brother."

Mac pauses. It's chilly in here. He keeps his coat and hat on. "You mean I can't stay."

"I mean I think you should talk to your brother." Stan gestures at the towel-rod spear in Mac's hand. "What the hell is that?"

Mac looks at it. "It's just — it's just — " He looks back up. "You mean I can't stay."

Stan gets up. "Call your brother." He goes to the door, where he says, "And turn up the damn heat! It's freezing in here."

When Stan has gone, Mac turns up the heat, but he doesn't turn on any lights. He sits at a desk that looks out across the intersection. Darkness has fallen, and heavy snowflakes are tumbling in the streetlights. The city is quiet. Even through the closed window, he can hear the traffic signal chirping.

On a late afternoon in Paris, in August of 1999, he had sat in a little park called Les Arènes de Lutèce. This was the ancient arena of Lutetia, as the Romans called their little settlement on the Seine. There wasn't much in the way of ruins, just a sandy space in the circular shape of the old arena and a crumbling curved wall on one side. There was a metal historical marker he couldn't read. The park wasn't mentioned in his tourist guide; he had just happened on it as he wandered. He was in Paris because Ruth had received a travel grant from the university and shoehorned him into her trip. They weren't married yet. They had been together for just six months, and both of them knew, although nobody said it, that this trip was a test of their future.

On this particular afternoon, Ruth had said they should have some alone time. She went off to see an "eco quarter" where they were implementing changes that she hoped to bring to Burlington. Mac had walked off without a plan, partly because he knew how this scandalized Ruth, who loved to map out every moment of her day. And he had wound up on a green bench in this little park, watching people walk across its sunny open space. A fortyish couple pushing a stroller. A young woman in a tight-fitting top, flashing several inches of bare midriff above her jeans. An older man in a fedora, using a cane to pick his way around the periphery, passing behind Mac's bench and then around the circle again. Mac imagined men in togas seated on tiers of stone seats, watching men in loin cloths who fought until one of them couldn't fight anymore. Two sets of church bells pealed in succession, gently quarreling over the time. The old man crossed his field of vision again. Above the neighboring buildings, a lemon-yellow sunset faded, tender and precise as a Bach cello suite. He and Ruth were embarking on something enormous, which she already bore in her body, although they didn't know that yet. The potential for failure was terrifying. But it was bracing, too.

In class on Monday, Kevin tells them about overshoot. In any ecosystem, he says, when a population exceeds the carrying capacity of the area—that is, its ability to support the consumption of its resources—this leads to a die-off of the population. It's a law of nature. If leopards consume too much prey in their region, fewer leopards will survive. If spiders eat all the local flies, the spiders will die back, until there is equilibrium again.

Until about 1970, Kevin says, the Earth was more or less in balance, producing enough to support the consumption of its resources. But the human population kept growing, and its demands kept increasing. Soon, we were exhausting resources more quickly than they could be replenished. By the turn of this century, we were using the equivalent of 1.5 Earths, and the deficit keeps growing.

Harper raises her hand. Kevin looks surprised. But he can't not call on her.

"People don't think that way," she says.

"What do you mean?"

"I mean, people go to the store, and there's food. They go to the filling station, and there's gas. As long as they have money, there's enough. They're not in overshoot."

Kevin gestures to his PowerPoint. "But the whole system," he says. "The whole system can't sustain this kind of consumption."

"Yes, it can. Until it can't. And then we'll figure out another way." She's not even sure she believes this, but it feels good.

"By then it will be too late."

"Too late for what?"

"The system will collapse."

"You mean there will be a die-off?"

"Yes." He checks his watch. The hour is almost over.

"So who dies off?"

"Well—"

"It's not going to be the rich people, right? Or the college professors."

The girl next to Harper inhales sharply. Kevin looks at his watch again, and says, "That's all the time we have today. We can pick this up tomorrow."

Harper doesn't want to pick it up tomorrow. She wants to save some trees today. She gets out of the classroom as quickly as she can, and, seeing the downtown bus approaching, runs to catch it.

When the bus stops at the medical center, she steps off. She doesn't know why, exactly. Her mother isn't there today. Ruth would be on campus now, in a classroom of her own, carrying on as if there were no problem with her health.

Harper enters the hospital at an automatic revolving door that sweeps her into the entrance hall. It's a vast space, three stories high, with a curving wall of glass panels that keep it bright even on a cloudy winter day. This section of the medical center was grafted onto the older buildings not long ago, giving the whole complex the look of a mid-sized airport. Once, after she had visited a friend with a skiing injury, her father arranged to pick her up out front by saying, "I'll meet you at Departures."

Today the hall thrums with activity—green-vested volunteers at the information desk; orderlies standing behind discharged patients in wheelchairs, waiting for rides; friends and family in armchairs, leafing through old home-improvement magazines. The murmur of a dozen muffled conversations hovers in the air.

On second thought, Harper does know why she's here: this place comforts her. Everyone is vulnerable, everyone's a geek. Here, they don't have to pretend.

Making her way downstairs to a food kiosk, she gets herself a bagel. She slices it in the little guillotine, then pops the halves into a toaster. Over at the cream-and-sugar counter, she sees the charge nurse from the other day. Brisk as ever, she is filling a cardboard tray with coffees made to order. She nods at Harper with a smile, then heads off down the hall.

A tall thought rises in Harper's mind. Next semester she can sign up for Biology.

When she walks into Knead that afternoon for a cup of coffee before work, there's no avoiding him. Because there he is, his lanky legs tucked under the little table. His sandy hair is longer than it was five years ago, and also thinner; his bald spot is closer to a tonsure now. She feels a pang of sympathy: he was always vain about it.

She could turn and leave—but what good would that do? She'd just encounter him again.

He doesn't look surprised. He rises from his seat, but seems to know that a hug would be too much. With a little noncommittal smile, he gestures to the other chair.

But she doesn't sit. She walks up close, so she won't have to raise her voice. She can smell his aftershave.

"You have to leave," she says.

And then, before he can say a word, she walks out. She doesn't need that coffee anyway. As she steps onto the sidewalk, it occurs to her that this could be the last time she will ever see him. But then, she thinks, that's true for everybody, all the time.

There's a crust of snow left over from last night, like fake snow on a movie set. Across the street, the swastika still glares from the temple door. When she steps into Pho Hong, Josie is topping up sauces at the tables, and Jimmy's fulminating to her through the order window about the latest crazy tweet from Trump. At ten till five, it's fully dark outside, and the big garage-door windows reflect the brightness within, the warmth of a winter restaurant. Some early birds have gathered at the door. It's going to be a busy night. Harper doesn't try to say how glad she is to be here.

Fomite

About Fomite

A fomite is a medium capable of transmitting infectious organisms from one individual to another.

"The activity of art is based on the capacity of people to be infected by the feelings of others." Tolstoy, *What Is Art?*

Writing a review on Amazon, Good Reads, Shelfari, Library Thing or other social media sites for readers will help the progress of independent publishing. To submit a review, go to the book page on any of the sites and follow the links for reviews. Books from independent presses rely on reader-to-reader communications.

For more information or to order any of our books, visit:
http://www.fomitepress.com/

More Titles from Fomite...

Novels

Fomite

Scott Archer Jones — *A Rising Tide of People Swept Away*
Julie Justicz — *Degrees of Difficulty*
Maggie Kast — *A Free Unsullied Land*
Darrell Kastin — *Shadowboxing with Bukowski*
Coleen Kearon — *#triggerwarning*
Coleen Kearon — *Feminist on Fire*
Jan English Leary — *Thicker Than Blood*
Diane Lefer — *Confessions of a Carnivore*
Rob Lenihan — *Born Speaking Lies*
Douglas W. Milliken — *Our Shadows' Voice*
Colin Mitchell — *Roadman*
Ilan Mochari — *Zinsky the Obscure*
Peter Nash — *Parsimony*
Peter Nash — *The Perfection of Things*
George Ovitt — *Stillpoint*
George Ovitt — *Tribunal*
Gregory Papadoyiannis — *The Baby Jazz*
Pelham — *The Walking Poor*
Andy Potok — *My Father's Keeper*
Frederick Ramey — *Comes a Time*
Joseph Rathgeber — *Mixedbloods*
Kathryn Roberts — *Companion Plants*
Robert Rosenberg — *Isles of the Blind*
Fred Russell — *Rafi's World*
Ron Savage — *Voyeur in Tangier*
David Schein — *The Adoption*
Lynn Sloan — *Principles of Navigation*
L.E. Smith — *The Consequence of Gesture*
L.E. Smith — *Travers' Inferno*
L.E. Smith — *Untimely RIPped*
Bob Sommer — *A Great Fullness*
Tom Walker — *A Day in the Life*
Susan V. Weiss —*My God, What Have We Done?*
Peter M. Wheelwright — *As It Is On Earth*
Suzie Wizowaty — *The Return of Jason Green*

Poetry
Anna Blackmer — *Hexagrams*
Antonello Borra — *Alfabestiario*
Antonello Borra — *AlphaBetaBestiaro*
Antonello Borra — *Fabbrica delle idee/The Factory of Ideas*
L. Brown — *Loopholes*
Sue D. Burton — *Little Steel*
Christine Butterworth-McDermott — *Evelyn As*
David Cavanagh— *Cycling in Plato's Cave*
James Connolly — *Picking Up the Bodies*

Fomite

Fomite

Fomite

Peter Schumann — *Diagonal Man, Volumes One and Two*
Peter Schumann — *Faust 3*
Peter Schumann — *Planet Kasper, Volumes One and Two*
Peter Schumann — *We*

Plays
Stephen Goldberg — *Screwed and Other Plays*
Michele Markarian — *Unborn Children of America*

Essays
Robert Sommer — *Losing Francis: Essays on the Wars at Home*

Made in the USA
Monee, IL
26 May 2020